In all the time she and Kate were lovers this had never happened. Kate had never touched anything, changed anything. She had never intruded on Amanda's life in any way.

Shaken, Amanda returned to the sitting room to find Debby on the sofa calmly reading a magazine. She looked up, eyes dark with promise, and, halfway between rage and desire, Amanda walked over and removed the magazine from her hands.

Without a word, she pulled Debby to her feet and immediately slid a hand up her dress, past her perfect thighs into the damp space between them. Really sophisticated. Stifling Debby's small startled gasp with her mouth, Amanda kissed her hard and passionately. Then she carried her into the bedroom, dumped her unceremoniously on the bed and rolled on top of her.

As she dragged Debby's dress off, stared worshipfully at her immaculate form and buried her face in those astounding breasts, Amanda knew she was in trouble.

INTRODUCING AMANDA VALENTINE

BY ROSE BEECHAM

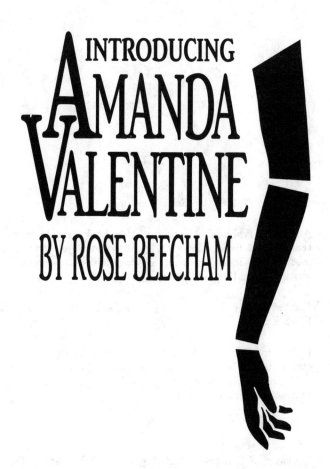

INTRODUCING AMANDA VALENTINE

BY ROSE BEECHAM

The Naiad Press, Inc.
1992

Printed in the United States of America on acid-free paper
First Edition

Edited by Claire McNab and Katherine V. Forrest
Cover design by Pat Tong and Bonnie Liss
   (Phoenix Graphics)
Typeset by Sandi Stancil

Library of Congress Cataloging-in-Publication Data

Beecham, Rose. 1958–
   Introducing Amanda Valentine / by Rose Beecham.
      p.   cm.
   ISBN 1-56280-021-3 : $9.95
   I. Title.
PR9639.3.B344I57   1992
823--dc20   92-19092
                                                                    CIP

For Steve

*A pat on the hand is worth
two manuscripts in the bin.*

Acknowledgments

The Wellington Central CIB has my everlasting gratitude for making my police research fun as well as gritty. I am indebted to Claire McNab and Katherine Forrest for their advice and discerning editing; to Steve Danby and Janette Day for their enthusiastic support; and to Greer Harding for the use of her appearance. Lastly I thank my family for being there, always.

CHAPTER ONE

It was 2:00 AM when the phone jolted Amanda into consciousness. She grunted a hello and swung her legs out of the bed. Hot sheet clung damply to her thighs.

"Who's that?" she mumbled, still half asleep.

"It's me. Jezebel."

"What's up?"

"I'm in some trouble, lovie." The contralto voice broke into a hoarse baritone. "Got me some rough trade."

"Where are you?" Amanda ripped open a drawer. Cradling the receiver between ear and shoulder, she struggled into jeans and a T-shirt.

"My place."

"Vivian Street?"

"Yeah. But I gotta get out. They'll be back. I know it."

"They? Who?" Amanda groped around in the darkness for her holster.

The phone crackled with harsh sobs. "Honey, I gotta talk to you."

There was a stirring from her bed and Amanda glanced over her shoulder. Kate mumbled then retreated back into unconsciousness.

"Have you put the squeeze on someone again, Jezebel?" Amanda demanded angrily.

Jezebel moaned. "Please. Just come. Marion. The car-park."

Amanda hesitated. The Marion Street parking lot was a hangout for itinerant hookers, street kids and small-time dope dealers. It was Jezebel's turf. "You being followed?"

"Did Jesus mount an ass?"

"Jezebel, who are they?"

More sobbing. "Can't talk now. Please, doll."

"Okay. I'll be there in ten minutes. Wait at the burger bar then walk 'round."

The phone clicked. Amanda buttoned her jeans, pulled on a pair of Nikes, stole a quick guilty look at Kate, then slipped out of her room.

In the rush hour, Marion Street was a twenty-minute drive from Amanda's Mount Vic townhouse. With the streets empty of commuters,

2

she reached the parking lot in five, killed her lights and pulled up just inside the entrance. Apart from a solitary hooker in pink hot pants, there was no one around. Even lowlife had to sleep sometime.

Amanda opened her door, hoping for a drift of cool air. It was the hottest January in fifty years. Celibacy weather, she thought wryly. Fanning herself with a restless hand, she stared toward the corner where Marion connected with Vivian Street.

The minutes ticked by. The streetwalker with the hot pants emerged from her doorway and got into a car. Out of habit Amanda ran a make and jotted down a description of the john. She heard voices, a bottle smashing. Somewhere in the parking lot a cat yowled. There was no sign of Jezebel.

Amanda fired up the Toyota and turned onto Vivian Street. The place tried hard to pass as a red-light district; a few run-down strip joints, the usual peep shows and triple XXX cinemas, massage parlors, a hairdresser with its front window boarded up, a kitsch shop specializing in fripperies for the local queens, and Jimmy's Burger Bar. It was a preschool playground compared with anything Stateside.

She cruised slowly then pulled up at Jimmy's and poked her head out into the heavy air. "Jezebel been here tonight?"

The small Chinese man at the street front counter shook his head. "Not tonight. You wanna fries? Ice cream?"

"Later, maybe." With a leaden feeling in her stomach, Amanda started up the hill.

* * * * *

3

Jezebel's was a ground floor flat in a decrepit colonial mansion. The place was in total darkness. Amanda loosened her jacket and approached the sole wooden door. It was swinging on its hinges. Tracing her fingers along the wooden jamb, she located the evidence of a forced entry.

Instantly, she flattened herself against the wall and pulled her Smith & Wesson. With a cautious foot, she nudged the door wide. A loud creak was swallowed without trace by the torpid night. Amanda felt a trickle of sweat escape from between her breasts and collect on her T-shirt, gluing it to her midriff.

She slipped inside the door and paused for a split second to get her bearings. There wasn't a sound. Adrenalin pumping, she advanced toward a room on her right. The sitting room, she recalled from previous visits.

She took a step back, delivered a swift kick to the door and shouted, "Police. Freeze."

Nothing moved. Swinging the gun left and right, she eased into the room, checked behind the door, flicked on the light switch. A single red lamp feebly lifted the gloom.

Amanda stood stock still. The place was totaled, the heavy deco sofa and chairs overturned, upholstery slashed, horsehair and cotton spilling out. The floor was a sea of upended drawers, smashed ornaments and overturned potted plants. The only things left untouched were the china ducks flying across the opposite wall. Beside them a floral curtain stirred in front of a tall sash window.

"Jezebel?" Amanda murmured and began picking

her way through the wreckage. Something tripped her, and cursing, she peered down at a dark object. A crowbar. She resisted the urge to pick it up, this time surveying the room more urgently.

A door to one side was open. She went in fast, trigger-finger poised. Then she saw her. Stretched out on the floor beside the bed, a phone cradled in her awkwardly bent arms. The cord had been severed.

"Jezebel!" She bent low over the prone figure and gasped with horror. A split second later professional detachment shut a blind on her feelings. Someone had taken a club to Jezebel, pulped her face, broken her arms and God knew what else.

"Jezebel. It's me. Amanda Valentine. Who did this to you?"

She placed her ear immediately above the bloodied lips. Jezebel emitted a groan. She was alive but barely conscious.

Amanda cupped her shoulders. "Jezebel!"

There was no response. Shaking, she radioed for an ambulance and back-up, then settled down beside her favorite street source, willing her to live.

Tears pricked her eyes and her throat was dry and strained. Damn Jezebel! There was only one explanation for this. She was up to her old tricks again. Blackmail.

Her mind raced on. Jezebel must have come home, found the place wrecked and phoned Amanda. And she knew they'd be back. How? They were after something of course. Photos . . . Bring the john home, camera on automatic, get him blindfolded . . . They hadn't found what they wanted when they tossed the place first time 'round, so they'd waited outside for Jezebel to show, gained entrance, and beaten the shit out of her to make her talk.

Hearing sirens whooping their way up the hill, Amanda let go of Jezebel's hand and returned to the shambles of the sitting room. Moments later car doors were slamming out on the street and a swarm of cops and medics invaded the flat, Detective Sergeant Joe Moller loping along behind them.

Amanda sighed with relief at the sight of her one-time partner. Joe was a big man, the kind of cop you expect to see on TV; mid-forties, greying pepper-colored hair, well-scrubbed face. A few years back he might have been called a hunk, but these days he was carrying too much surplus. Joe blamed it all on marital complacency. Amanda thought it was pizza.

He spotted her and pushed his way over. "What've we got, mate?"

Stiff-lipped, Amanda led him into Jezebel's room to see for himself.

"Christ," he muttered. "No oil painting."

The medics were shoving a drip into one of Jezebel's arms. Amanda crouched down beside her and said huskily, "It's okay, Jezebel, the ambulance is here and I'm taking you to the hospital now."

Jezebel's breathing was wet and shallow. Ribs. They'd really worked her over. She must have dragged herself into her bedroom once they'd gone, tried to phone for help. But they'd cut the cord, hadn't they. These boys watched TV.

Amanda touched Jezebel's shoulder. "I'm gonna get them," she whispered.

There was a faint hiss and Amanda bent lower. "I'm listening, Jezebel," she urged.

The bloody lips struggled to emit a sound. Slivers of broken tooth emerged. Jezebel managed one word before she lost consciousness. "Hippo."

"You reckon it could have been a queer bashing?" Joe asked a couple of hours later, driving home from the hospital.

Amanda flinched. "I doubt it. I think she's been up to her old tricks again."

"Blackmail?"

"Probably."

"So we gotta find names and numbers for all her johns. She must have some kind of diary. You never saw anyone?"

"I wish ..." If only she'd gone straight 'round there. She must have missed them by minutes.

"What was she saying back there?"

Amanda frowned. "It was hard to make out. But I think she said 'Hippo.'"

They pulled up outside her place and Amanda's stomach knotted at the sight of Kate's car. She was dreading the confrontation she sensed was brewing. It wouldn't be the first time a lover had delivered that ultimatum — it's me or the job.

Joe licked a stubby finger and held it to the morning air. "Never thought I'd be sorry to see the sun rise. Feel that. It's almost cool."

Amanda stared up as they got out of the car. The sky was oyster colored, pink at the edges.

"Ricky Hippolyte," she said, glancing at the big man beside her. "They call him Hippo on Vivian Street."

Joe raised his bushy salt-and-pepper brows. "You know the guy?"

"I put him away on a heroin rap a couple of years back. He's been out on parole three months."

"Trick of Jezebel's?"

Amanda shook her head. "Not Ricky. He's just another punk."

"Suspect then?"

Amanda frowned. Ricky couldn't handle violence. She could remember him cowering in the cells, vomiting when another inmate's nose was broken in a brawl. Inside he'd stayed away from trouble. Got himself some muscle-bound protection the usual way. He'd never have worked Jezebel over himself, she was convinced of that.

"I don't think he's our perpetrator, Joe," she said, "but maybe he knows something."

"Okay. So I find the kid and bring him in. You want to be cut in on this one, right?"

"I owe Jezebel," Amanda said with feeling. It was Jezebel who had risked her hide as bait in the Sauna Strangler case.

"Yeah. I know."

They fell silent. Amanda suspected they were both probably remembering the same freeze frame — Jezebel hanging out the second-story window as they burst in on the strangler with his hands around her throat.

"Hang fire on Hippolyte for the moment," Amanda said distractedly.

Joe's brow puckered. "If he's a witness . . ."

Amanda sighed. The first twenty-four hours. The

critical time after a crime is committed. She lifted a weary hand to her forehead and wiped off the sweat. "Can you bear with me? I have a hunch."

He treated her to a long-suffering look and rearranged his shirt over his spreading stomach. "A hunch. Sure, Inspector Valentine. I don't have a problem with that." With a speaking glance, he turned toward the patrol car that had followed them.

Amanda figured he was probably repeating some mens' group mantra about hearing what women are saying.

CHAPTER TWO

It was no way to spend a night, Amanda reflected over her morning caffeine a few hours later. Kate was still sleeping, and, delaying the inevitable, Amanda had avoided waking her. Instead she'd snatched a couple of precious hours to scan a week of unread newspapers.

Her throat tightened and for a moment she hated herself. Why couldn't she be in love with Kate, change her job, get her kicks like other people? What had she become? Some kind of thrills junkie, a weapons nut? Was hers the kind of personality that she, lacking a job, would parade around the streets in a borrowed uniform and shoot up the local school with an AK47 the day a shop assistant forgot to say hello?

The polite trill of the doorbell jerked her from her navel gazing. Irritably, she glanced at her watch. It was probably the graveyard shift paying calls on the way home. Eight-thirty on a Saturday morning. She'd barely finished dressing, she'd had three hours sleep and she was about to be dumped by her lover. Perfect timing, thanks guys.

Scowling, she trudged down the passage and hauled open the door. Decorating her porch like blowflies crowding a corpse was a TV crew, cameras poised and jeans indecently tight.

Some bimbo in nightclub gear fronted up with a toothy smile and shoved her foot in the door. Her face was vaguely familiar. "Inspector Valentine?" she breathed.

Her perfume almost knocked Amanda out. Obsession; she'd know it anywhere. "Yes. What —"

"Thank you." The blonde made a signal over her shoulder.

Checking their zippers, the crew strutted into position. Amanda caught another flash of orthodontry and the blonde whispered, "Would you mind stepping out a little further for the boys?"

With an unexpectedly firm grip, she seized Amanda's arm and propelled her into full view. "Thank you." She said it as if Amanda had just given her a million dollars.

"Look, I don't know what all this is about but I have no comment and —" That was as far as she got.

"We're rolling, Inspector Valentine," the blonde said sweetly and thrust a bulbous mike in her face. "Hello, New Zealand," she greeted her public while Amanda took in the full horror of the situation. "I'm Debby Daley and this week I'm introducing Amanda Valentine."

"There must be some mistake," Amanda tried again. The Debby Daley Show was a prime time celebrity talk show with a huge following among the great unwashed. Its guests were politicians, tycoons and the bizarre. Amanda supposed she might fit in the third category.

"No mistake," Debby assured her, smile firmly in place. "Now we *are* filming, Inspector Valentine ... may I call you Amanda — off-camera, that is?"

Amanda gazed into the camera and, mentally shaking herself, managed to transform her expression from annoyance to calm authority. These days, she avoided dealing with the media, assigning a senior detective the task of answering the usual mindless questions that came with the territory in homicide investigations.

But this was different. The Debby Daley Show was not a thirty-second news spot. You got a whole twenty minutes to make an ass of yourself, Amanda thought cheerlessly.

"Inspector Valentine has been with the New Zealand police force for the past five years," Debby announced. "She is responsible for solving numerous serious crimes. Only six weeks ago she led the daring daytime raid that resulted in the arrest of the Lucy Chan kidnappers. Inspector —" She drew a little closer, her expression that of a woman longing to be impressed. "You were recently promoted to your current rank and now for your bravery in rescuing little Lucy Chan from that burning barn you've just been awarded a Queen's Gallantry Medal in the New Year's Honours List. How do you feel?"

Embarrassed. Guilty as hell. "Naturally I'm very honored," Amanda replied tepidly. "This award reflects not only my work but that of the Police Force as a whole. On that basis I'm proud to accept it." Shameless, she thought and met Debby's wide aquamarine eyes.

They were regarding her with undisguised amusement. Evidently Debby Daley found her loyalty to the Force funny, Amanda thought, niggled.

"Inspector." Debby assumed a confiding tone. "You worked for the New York Police Department before coming to little New Zealand. Are criminals on this side of the world easier to catch?"

"Criminals are never easy to catch, Debby," Amanda returned coolly. "But fortunately for the public, members of *my* profession are not employed solely for their pretty faces."

Debby didn't even blink. The irony had slipped straight past her, Amanda observed. Hardly surprising, of course. The woman was obviously suffering a chronic case of airheadedness. No one could be that blonde. The hair had to be dyed. And those breasts ... Her attention strayed momentarily to Debby's plunging neckline. Silicone; they had to be. Probably the nipples as well.

She lifted her gaze and found Debby gazing at her expectantly, evidently waiting for an answer to something. Irritated at this uncharacteristic lapse in her concentration, Amanda fudged, "Could you repeat that question please?"

There was a split second's hesitation, then Debby bailed her out, sweet-voiced. "I was observing, given what you just said, Inspector, that you must find it quite a dilemma being New Zealand's most glamorous detective."

Amanda groaned inwardly. The media's preoccupation with her appearance infuriated her, but she couldn't afford to show it. Forcing a light note, she replied, "I can think of worse problems."

Debby offered an understanding smile. "Inspector, your work exposes you to the very *worst* crimes ... brutal murders, rapes and beatings. I wonder, what is the big attraction for you in being a detective?"

Amanda found herself giving a double take. The question was nothing new ... *What's a nice girl like you doing in a job like this?* But for some reason Debby's studied artlessness unnerved her.

"There are many satisfying aspects to my job," she said, conscious of the slight hesitance that had given away her discomfort. "I enjoy being part of a team, every case is a challenge. And I like hard work."

"How do your colleagues react to having a woman in charge?"

"Why not ask them?"

"Have you ever experienced discrimination against you as a woman?"

"Only when the media asks me questions they would not ask a man."

Their eyes locked for a moment and Amanda felt a flare of satisfaction. Debby hadn't missed that one.

"The Police Force has seemed slow to promote

women into senior positions." Debby's voice abruptly lost its girlish edge. "As an Inspector, are you merely a token woman?"

Amanda raised her eyebrows, not about to be provoked. "I think I've earned my rank on merit, Debby."

Debby smiled, but the warmth did not extend to her eyes. "Well, your record is certainly a demonstration of that." Pitching a serious look into the cameras, she prattled on about the Tunnel Rapist, the Stacey Roberts case, the Sauna Strangler. Doubtless they would run the voice-over with the customary lurid footage, Amanda thought.

"Presently you are leading the Garbage Dump Killer inquiry," Debby pressed on, her blitheness recaptured. "What do you think we're dealing with here, Inspector? We've got bits of body being dug up by sanitation workers, unidentified victims . . . How many are there?"

"Body parts?"

"Victims."

"Three so far." Minus a head, a torso and assorted limbs.

"So far," Debby pounced. "Are you saying he's going to kill again?"

Cursing the careless slip, Amanda took a deep calming breath and counted to three. The Police Commissioner had ordered them to play down the possibility that they were dealing with a serial killer. Repeat murder was virtually unheard of in New Zealand, where most killings could be filed under the heading "domestic." Undue media attention would only succeed in terrorizing the public and bringing all sorts of crazies out of the woodwork to waste everyone's time.

"We are attempting to identify three bodies," Amanda said succinctly. "That's all I can tell you."

Debby beamed. The boys moved in for a close-up. "I know it's police policy not to scare the public with speculation about serial killers, Inspector, but maybe you could tell us whether you've investigated such crimes in the United States."

A small tremor snaked down Amanda's spine. Did the Garbage Dump Killer watch the Debby Daley Show? Would he be sitting in front of his television laughing at her while a severed head drained in his fridge? She paled slightly and snapped, "I was involved in several inquiries in New York."

"Can you tell us something about the kind of person who commits such horrific crimes?"

No comment, Amanda thought. *Change the subject.* Instead she said, "We know from psychological profiles that in the United States, at least, the serial killer is typically a male in his thirties, usually considered by others to be a very private person. He was probably cruel to animals as a child, he may have suffered sexual abuse . . ." Just for him, she added recklessly, "They always slip up sometime because they can't resist showing off. You could say they are more egotistical than intelligent. But being that way, of course, they believe they're the opposite."

Debby was staring at her. She seemed about to say something when her attention was arrested by a movement behind them.

"What are you doing?" a sleepy voice asked, and

Amanda turned in time to see a small, pink-cheeked woman framed in the doorway. She was wearing a lavender nightshirt that proclaimed *Women Do It Better.*

"Kate!" Amanda gasped. "Get inside." Wildly conscious of the camera recording her every move, she hustled her lover into the house.

"What on earth are they doing here?" Kate demanded as the door shut behind them.

"It's Debby Daley," Amanda groaned. "I'm being interviewed for that ridiculous show of hers."

"Looks like you'll be tied up for a while then," Kate said dully. "I guess I'd better be going."

There was a sharp rap at the door and Amanda shouted, "Hold on a minute."

Kate was already walking away.

"I'll get rid of them," Amanda said. "Please stay, Kate. We need to talk."

Kate shook her coppery head. "I'd rather not. I feel stupid enough already. Go back out and give them their pound of flesh. I'll ring you later."

"No," Amanda began. "Kate, I —"

The doorbell shrilled insistently.

"Amanda, don't make this any harder. Even if we did talk, what would be the point? There's no easy way to say goodbye." With a brief look of regret, she turned sharply and walked away.

CHAPTER THREE

Jezebel was in a room of her own at the Public Hospital. Despite the huge bunch of flowers on the bedside table, the place smelled of disinfectant and linoleum wax. Commercial blooms, Amanda reminded herself; they bred the scent out of them.

Apart from the police guard at the door, there were two other people in the room, a nurse and a doctor. The doctor hovered beside the bed, surveying its contents with a look of distaste. He was a pale man, mid-thirties, well-scrubbed. Even in a white coat and latex gloves he managed to look preppie.

Amanda flashed her ID at him. It earned her a look of amused tolerance.

"Nasty job for a lady. Nurse! X-rays." He held out his hand like a spoiled schoolboy.

The nurse moved around Amanda to reach for a pile of envelopes directly in front of him.

He examined the x-rays, wandered through the charts, then smiled liplessly at a spot on the wall behind Amanda's shoulder.

"How is she?" Amanda asked.

"She?" He lifted a disdainful brow.

"Jezebel. Your patient." She adopted the careful delivery one would normally reserve for yokels or the criminally insane.

"I believe the patient is listed as a *Mr.* Heemi Matenga," the doctor drawled in a nasal tone.

"So how is *she?*" Amanda repeated. Anger pulsed hotly through her limbs. Jezebel was barely recognizable, her face a mishmash of swelling and sutures, her body bound like a mummy and her head shaved across one side where blood was caked around a deep laceration. She was still unconscious.

The doctor's jumpy blue eyes flicked from the chart to the bed. "The patient regained consciousness very briefly this afternoon."

"Did she say anything?"

He threw Amanda a supercilious look. "Nothing intelligible."

"Do I take it that she said something but your staff was not certain what?" Amanda said quietly.

The doctor shrugged. "My staff is on the hospital's payroll, Miss Valentine, not yours."

Amanda got to her feet, pleased in a petty kind of way that she was taller than he. "That's Inspector

Valentine," she told him softly. "And unless I'm mistaken this hospital is a publicly funded facility. That makes you an employee of the taxpayer, at least for the few hours you manage to drag yourself away from private practice to work here. In the interests of your employers, I'm telling you to record everything this patient says. I don't give a damn whether it's intelligible or not. Is that clear?"

His Adam's apple bobbed and a slow flush crawled up his cheeks. He dropped the chart onto its hook at the end of the bed and started out the door.

"One more thing, doctor," Amanda called after him.

He glanced over his shoulder, eyes narrowed with hostility.

"Your patient's name is Jezebel. Got that?"

A few hours later, sitting at her table at home, Amanda shoved aside a pile of forensic reports and cradled her head in her hands. "Too hot for you, buddy?" she whispered beneath her breath. "Bet you're getting real restless. Bet you're out there somewhere tapping your barometer right about now. Bet your fridge is smelling real bad."

The Big Mack Task Force had been established nearly three months ago to investigate the garbage dump killings, the investigation team acquiring its name after the occasion of the first limb discovered — a severed hand inside a McDonald's bag left on the bonnet of a Mack truck. The task force consisted of twenty detectives, fifteen of them Wellington based, the remainder scattered about the country.

They were working around the clock, yet Amanda felt as if they were moving backwards. She stared down at the latest analyses of data and wove her fingers restlessly into her hair. They had canvassed and recanvassed every house in the dump vicinity, interviewed every sanitation worker several times over, followed up every phone call, inspected the contents of one hell of a lot of suspicious smelling garbage bags reported by concerned citizens. And zilch. A big, fat nothing.

Of the three victims, two men and a woman, none had been identified, a fact Amanda found both infuriating and puzzling. How could three people disappear just like that with nobody noticing? The victims were connected only by their age, mid- to late-twenties, and race — they were all white. Needle tracks indicated 'Mary' was a heroin user. It was possible, probable even, that the killer sought out victims no one would miss. Addicts, prostitutes, homeless. But even throwaways had friends on the street . . . mothers somewhere.

Reconstruction was onerous without a scene or date of the killings, without witnesses and without a physical clue connecting any of the victims to an individual. Not a trace of fiber, not a print, not a hair. The only conclusions the task force had arrived at were the obvious. The killer murdered his victims in enough privacy to attract no attention and then was able to dismember them and store them in a fridge or freezer for extended periods. In other words he lived alone or had sole use of a place where he could carry out his macabre rituals. He owned a car and, given the fact that all the limbs discovered so far were dumped in Wellington, it seemed likely that he lived in the city or its environs. That narrowed the search down to about 400,000 people.

Amanda wondered if the Garbage Dump Killer could somehow pick up her messages. Cosmic E-mail from Detective Inspector Amanda Valentine of the Wellington CIB. *I'm gonna get you, shitface.*

She glanced at her watch. Seven o'clock. Of course it was. She could smell scorched meat, couldn't she? Amanda stalked to her kitchen window and surveyed the neighbor's back yard. Yes, there it was. The genuine Kiwi Barbeque; sausages hissing, beer flowing, smoke rising. No hot Antipodean night was complete without one.

Listlessly, she opened the fridge and leaned into the cool blast. Madam immediately arrived at her feet, warbling a feline plea, and Amanda dragged out a bowl of steamed fish and offered it to the little tabby.

Madam's tail switched.

"I sweated for that cod," Amanda said. "Eat it, or I'll send you next door for some carcinogens."

She ladled a heap of coffee beans into the grinder, wallowing in olfactory pleasure as they were pulverized. Overhead, her ceiling fan halfheartedly stirred the thick air. Out in the street, someone yelled Happy New Year, a few days late.

Amanda poured the coffee and played back her answerphone messages.

Her mother calling from Hawaii. *Why don't you come on over, honey? You could do with a vacation.* Terrific. Three weeks of aerobics, sand in your mouth, and fighting off new age men on Kahuna trips. Who could ask for more?

Her father. *Great news about the medal. You still*

coming 'round this week? Sure, why not? Nothing like postmorteming every case with an armchair cop and having your nose rubbed in yet another theory about the Garbage Dump Killer.

Roseanne. *Can we have dinner sometime?*

The delicatessen. *Thanks for your order. There was no coffee. Did you forget?*

Kate, her voice stilted. *I left my sunglasses behind. Could you put them in the letterbox and I'll come past for them sometime?*

Amanda drained her coffee and poured a second cup. She could understand Kate not wanting to see her. Since they'd started dating six months back they'd spent only one whole weekend together. You couldn't choose when crime happened, but it bugged Amanda that it happened most Saturday nights.

At first, Kate had seemed fine about it. She was a busy person, a dedicated teacher and a keen tramper. And that was just as well, Amanda had often reflected. She needed a lover who didn't get underfoot.

Occasionally she fantasized about having a normal job: nine to five, catch the bus home, flowers for the little woman ... greeted at a suburban door with *Hi, honey, come and put your feet up while I make the coffee ...*

How did cops successfully avoid having their job impact on their personal life? You couldn't. She, of all people, should know that.

The phone rang. "I've located Hippolyte." It was Joe talking in between loud slurping noises. Coke, Amanda thought. In a can. No straw. "You want me to pick him up?"

"Not yet."

"Jesus, Amanda. If the punk did it we should try for a confession. We've got the crowbar."

"It's useless. Plastered with latents. Not a single match."

"He won't know that. C'mon, Amanda, we're pissing around."

"Trust me, Joe. I want you to watch him for a couple of days . . . see what he's up to."

There was a meaningful pause. "You're the boss. Wanna take a ride tonight — check him out?"

Amanda glanced morosely at her watch. It was only Saturday. Her first Saturday night off duty in a month.

"You got plans already?" Joe inquired.

"No," she said briskly. "Let's do it."

Ricky Hippolyte was staying at his sister's, a drab wooden house misplaced in the heart of yuppie country. The dump was an insult to its neighborhood. Its bilious green paintwork was flaked and uneven, a rusted-out car body decorated the front yard amidst a lush profusion of flowering weeds, and a homemade letterbox clung drunkenly to a tumble-down fence.

They'd been there five hours and apart from the thin wail of a baby executive, Delusion Grove was graveyard quiet. Lit up by the orange sodium street lamps it looked like a horror movie set; placid, smug suburbia lying in wait. *Nightmare on Delusion Grove.* Would anyone notice if Freddy meandered along here with a blood-drenched cleaver? Amanda doubted it.

Joe stroked his fleshy jowls and stretched his legs awkwardly in the cramped confines of the Ford mufti car. "You want something?" He shoved his hand into a vast lunch box behind his seat and produced a slab of cold pizza.

She eyed it warily and shook her head. "You have it."

"No sweat. There's plenty here. Homemade, too." He discarded the plastic wrapper and released the pungent odor of cheese, garlic and tomato.

Amanda took the offering and bit into it with queasy anticipation. A lump of congealed cheese and onion stuck to her teeth. She dislodged it with her thumb, commenting, "I'd forgotten surveillance was such a ball."

Joe glanced at her. "Yeah. It's been a while."

"I've missed it too," she said quietly. She and Joe had sat out some long nights together. Before she made Inspector.

"Looks like our boy's out partying," Joe observed. "Making up for lost time."

Ricky Hippolyte was only three months out of prison, but the working girls reckoned he was big time already. Bought doubles all 'round, wore a leather jacket and a diamond ring he'd actually paid for, drove a brand new Harley hog up and down ritzy Oriental Parade frightening the poodles. Amanda wondered where Ricky's new-found wealth was coming from. It had to be dope.

She'd asked around. A couple of streetwalkers reported seeing him with Jezebel in a white limo during the week before her "accident." No, they couldn't remember plates or nothing.

25

"You see the paper?" Joe grinned at her over the gory tableau of his pizza. In the half light it looked as though he were eating his hand.

Amanda shook her head.

"Got it here." He poked among the debris beside his seat and passed Amanda a crumpled newspaper.

She faced it into the streetlight. Under the banner headline GLAMOUR COP HONORED BY QUEEN was her mugshot. With a sigh of disgust, she tossed the paper back into his lap.

"You missed the best bit." Joe haw-hawed. *"Valentine, described by her superiors as Dirty Harry in a skirt, is rumored to operate a network of criminal informants equalled only by organized crime syndicates."*

"Yeah, and after hours I'm the tooth fairy." Amanda squirmed in her seat in a fruitless attempt to unglue her trousers from her thighs. *Dirty Harry in a skirt. Jesus.*

Joe wiped extraneous pizza off his mouth with a huge white handkerchief and read on. *"The sultry blonde is considered a role model for the modern professional woman ..."*

"What! Jesus. Who wrote that shit? I am not a goddamned blonde!" Amanda broke off at the sound of a motor thumping somewhere nearby.

A single headlight appeared at the end of Delusion Grove and they slid down their seats into what would appear from the outside to be a lover's embrace. The rest of Joe's pizza slid with them into the debris on the carpet.

"That's him," she whispered. Ricky Hippolyte was

looking as smooth as vegemite; black jeans, leather jacket, designer haircut. "And he's got company."

"Wheels?"

"Harley Davidson motorcycle. Personalized plate RUHOT. Looks like it gets to sleep indoors, too."

Joe groped for a pen, cursing under his breath. Amanda passed hers over and he started scribbling. "Companion?"

"Male Caucasian. Eighteen to twenty-five years. Five-ten, one-eighty pounds. Number two haircut. Jeans, Doc Marten boots. White T-shirt. Slight limp left leg."

"Know him?"

"No." Amanda eased the window down as the two men pushed the bike between the waist-high weeds and up the front steps. Their voices carried dully in the moist night air.

"This your old lady's place?"

"Nah, me sister's. She's in Oz . . ."

They disappeared into the house and five minutes later Delusion Grove reverberated to the latest from Guns N' Roses.

"For Chrissakes let's quick mucking around and pick up the little punk," Joe grumbled.

"Oh, sure," Amanda said tersely. "And what if he's dealing?"

"We hand him over to Vice when we've finished with him."

"Precisely. So we luck out on the Jezebel case and Bob Welch chalks up a clearance compliments of Amanda Valentine."

"Oh, now I get it!" Joe slapped his forehead

melodramatically. "It's all coming back to me. I should have guessed Welch would fit in somewhere."

"Give me a break," Amanda protested. "I'm not about to blow this case over some old grudge. There's something that bothers me about Hippolyte."

"Wanna share it with the group?"

"Remember I busted him back in 'eighty-eight while you were on secondment to Auckland?"

"Sure. You were under Welch, right?"

"Yes. And I'd only just started that investigation. Ricky was dealing — small time — and I was looking to track his supply lines. Before I could get to second base, Welch ordered the bust."

"Just like that?"

"I said we should string him along, see if we could build up to a major drop."

"But Welch wanted a quick clearance? It adds up. The guy was always a premature ejaculator."

Amanda winced. Obviously they hadn't made it as far as sensitive use of language in Joe's mens' group. "So we busted Hippolyte," she went on. "Real John Wayne stuff."

"Yeah, I gotcha. Now, what was that head- line . . ." Joe scratched his head then uttered a full-bodied laugh. "I remember — *Cover Girl Cop's Mammoth Bust.*"

"Thank you," Amanda said frostily. "Anyway, Welch had planned on interviewing Hippolyte himself, but he got called out on some Customs' seizure, so I took the statements. Hippolyte had some yuppie lawyer and the guy told him to make a full confession."

"Dumb advice."

"That's what I thought. There were a couple of weird things about that statement. The first was that Welch tore a piece out of me for getting it, acted like he'd been shot in the back."

"Ego problems," Joe inserted wisely.

"And Hippolyte kept raving on about how he'd been set up and this wasn't meant to happen."

Joe's eyes narrowed, registering an idea. "You think someone was handling protection for Hippolyte's bosses?"

"That was never an assigned case, Joe. I found out about Hippolyte by accident."

"And Welch ordered you to bust him before you could find out any more?"

"Maybe it was just coincidence. You know Bob's fanatical about clearing his desk. Hippolyte didn't know a thing. We got the conviction — small time supply — open-and-shut case. Keeps the brass happy."

"Smells bad to me," Joe commented. "Mr. Big gets to cover his tracks, someone upstairs makes a buck ..."

"We don't know that for sure."

"But maybe we can find out, huh. Let's talk to Hippolyte. No big deal. A few routine questions."

Amanda slid her fingers into her hair, prising it off her damp forehead. Routine questions ... no search, no bust. Bob Welch need never know. She opened her door. "Okay, let's do it."

Ricky Hippolyte answered the door, stared dazedly at their IDs, and extended his hands, palms up. "Hey man, I'm clean as — Watcha want?"

"May we come in for a moment, Ricky?" Amanda

lifted her voice over the pounding heavy metal rock. "We'd like to ask you a few routine questions."

Hippolyte slouched against the door jamb and eyed her suspiciously. "What's on ya mind, lady cop?"

"I don't like talking in doorways, Ricky."

"No one asked you here."

"It never cross your mind your neighbors might not share your taste in music?" Joe said, extracting his notebook. "Specially at two in the morning. Now . . . let me see. That's a Council noise ordinance you're violating. Then there's that wreck in your garden . . . you got an off-street permit for that?"

Hippolyte flung open the door. "Fuck off with that shit man! I never said ya couldn't come in." He led them along an unlit passageway to the source of the music, a semifurnished sitting room.

Hippolyte's guest was lounging back in a threadbare sofa, eyes closed, feet on a beer crate, a bottle in one hand and a joint in the other. On the wall behind him was a giant poster of *Iron Maiden* and a couple of centerfolds someone had drawn moustaches on.

"Home and garden," Joe muttered.

Ricky killed the sound and his buddy looked up with an expression of dull astonishment. Piggy eyes fastened on Amanda and the hand holding the joint flew instinctively beneath one thigh.

Joe grinned at him. "Pass it over, boy wonder."

"You got a search warrant?" Ricky brazened.

"You invited us in," Amanda said coolly. "Who's your friend?"

The friend looked twitchy.

"Mute, are we?" Joe snapped.

"Name's Dawson," Ricky supplied. "Sucker Dawson."

"When'dya get out?" Joe asked.

"Month ago," Ricky answered for him.

Joe stuck out his hand for the joint.

Sucker Dawson retrieved it from under his beefy thigh, then with a look of amoebic cunning, stuffed it into his mouth and swallowed it.

Joe shook his head slowly. "Room for dancing upstairs, ain't there, Dawson?"

The piggy eyes blinked.

Amanda surveyed the room. Crappy decor, naked lightbulbs, junk food wrappers. The place stank of vomit and cigarettes. Hippolyte evidently had better things to do than keep house. "Where were you between eleven and three last night, Ricky?" she asked.

Ricky shoved his thumbs into his belt, just along from the silver buckle of horses mating. "What's it to ya?"

"You can tell me here, or you can come on down to the station," she said benignly. "Your choice, Ricky."

He shuffled. "Last night ..." A sniff. "I was like ... er ... in bed."

Sucker Dawson started gouging at a pimple on his chin. He looked edgy. Typical ex-con nerves.

"In bed where?" Amanda prompted.

Ricky took out a comb and smoothed his hair back. "With a friend."

"His name and address?"

He jerked to attention, olive skin darkening. "Shit, man. I'm no fucking poofter."

"Name?"

Ricky paced, small agitated steps. "What the fuck is this?" he demanded. "I got rights too, ya know. Fucking harassment. That's what it is."

Amanda gave him a stony look. "I can get Joe here to shove his fingers down your mate's throat, and book you both for possession, or you can answer my questions, Ricky."

Sucker Dawson had slunk further and further into a corner of the sofa. Ricky muttered something about police violence, then he gave them the address of someone called Zanette. She was a singer, he emphasized, not some cheap slut either.

She was a stripper, Amanda deduced. "You know Jezebel Matenga?" she asked casually.

"Sure." Ricky's eloquent brown gaze dropped to the floor. "Who doesn't?"

He shuffled. Amanda gave him some silence, donned a small expectant smile. After a few seconds he couldn't stand it any longer and swung belligerent eyes to her face.

"What's she done?" The swagger fell short of convincing.

"Someone tried to kill her last night," said Amanda.

His face registered shock, then anger. It seemed authentic enough. "Kill her?" he echoed. "Who ..." Then he shut up.

"Did you do it, Ricky?"

"No fucking way! Jesus, man ..." He stuck out his chest, breathing hard. "You got nothing on me."

Joe eyeballed him like a gundog. "We got a weapon plastered with prints, sonny. You better hope none of them match yours."

Glass splintered behind them and they turned sharply. Sucker Dawson was staring sheepishly at a broken bottle and a pool of beer gathering around his feet.

"Well don't just stand there with your thumb up your bum," Joe told him. "Go get a cloth."

The youth boggled then pulled off his AC/DC T-shirt and dropped it into the dark liquid. A bundle of fat joints unravelled from one of the sleeves.

Joe picked them up and bagged them. "You want to press charges, Inspector?"

Amanda held Ricky's eyes, read the pleading. "That depends on what Ricky can tell us about Jezebel," she murmured.

"I already told ya," Ricky whined. "I don't know nothing."

Amanda stared at him intently, took the plastic bag off Joe and picked open one of the joints, revealing a matt of sticky heads. "Te Puke Thunder," she remarked. Very top drawer; the most expensive cannabis on the market. Grown mostly by organized crime, it was distributed by the biggest dealers in New Zealand — the "invisible men" at the top of the drug trade. "Where did you get this stuff?" she asked.

Both men were silent.

With a disinterested shrug, Amanda handed Hippolyte her card. "You think of anything about Jezebel, just give me a ring. Meantime we'll look after your gear."

As they left, she heard Ricky yelling at his

Neanderthal mate. *You fucking dickhead. Fucking put the rest of that shit down the bog before that bitch comes back.*

CHAPTER FOUR

On Sunday morning the sun rose at five-thirty. Amanda knew this because she'd forgotten to close her blinds when she fell into bed several hours earlier. Half-asleep, her body sticky and unwashed, she got up, jerked the curtains closed then dragged herself back between her damp sheets. Two restless hours later the phone rang.

"This is our lucky day," Joe informed her. "One double shift, a break between shifts of less than six hours, two unrostered shifts ... I'm talking thirty hours double time here."

"Thank you," Amanda managed over her furry tongue. "Is there something you need to tell me or can I go back to sleep now?"

There was a mumbling sound at the other end.

Amanda pushed her hair out of her eyes and elbowed herself upright. "Bacon and eggs?" she ventured.

"With some kind of special sauce," Joe said happily. "Dutch or something."

"Hollandaise." Amanda sighed. Eggs Benedict. "Could I buy Meryl off you, Joe?"

He laughed, called out something with his hand over the mouthpiece, then told Amanda, "Meryl says go find your own. Anyway," he went on, "the DSS just called. Wants me to pick you up. Harry Nepia's got something down Happy Valley."

"A head?" Amanda lurched to her feet.

"Don't know. Harry says some dame . . . er, woman . . . lets her dog out of the car and straightaway it starts whimpering and digging in some bags. She goes over and gets all hysterical. Saw a hand poking out."

"Anyone call McDougall?"

"Yeah, but she's in Taupo. Wilderness fishing, lucky stiff."

"Damn it. I don't want anyone else. Not after the last time." Some flunkey had bagged an arm, failing to notice that the wristwatch clinging to it had dropped off. There had almost certainly been a print there. Moira McDougall had noted it during the site inspection. "How long will it take to get her here?"

"There's an Army chopper going in," Joe said. "Three hours minimum, that's if they can find her."

"Terrific," she groaned. "You got an oxygen mask?"

In some countries people go to church on Sundays. In New Zealand they go to the dump. By the time Amanda and Joe got there, hundreds of cars were already coagulating on the dusty tip face. Harry Nepia, the Dump Supervisor, had done his best to cordon off the area. His staff had positioned a line of sixty-gallon drums so as to restrict cars to the opposite end of the dumping zone and the first cops on the scene had fenced off the evidence with yards of white tape. Uniform constables stood guard along the perimeters, supervised by a sergeant who repeatedly told curious onlookers to move on, there was nothing to see.

These countermeasures did little to deter the public. They were simply abandoning their cars in the permitted zone and swarming all over the garbage like confused ants, trying to get close enough to glimpse what was beyond the police barriers.

Amanda surveyed the spectacle with a sinking heart. "Jesus," she muttered to Joe. "Can't we get these rubber-neckers the hell out of here?"

"It's Sunday," Joe pointed out.

The sun was still mercifully low in the sky but that didn't make a whole lot of difference to the evil stench of the place. Two weeks of heatwave had extracted its price. Clouds of gritty dust swirled high in the air, constantly churned up by the vehicles

37

coming and going. It clung to everything; skin, hair, clothing. It got inside orifices, under eyelids and fingernails. And it tasted real bad.

"I hate this fucking place," Joe muttered. "Talk about the asshole of Wellington."

Amanda made the mistake of wiping her sweaty palms on her pants, contributing a fresh coating of grime. "You don't have to stay," she said. Joe was not officially assigned to the garbage dump inquiry. Knowing the toll the Sauna Strangler case had taken on his marriage, Amanda had deliberately passed over him. "I'll hang around till the DSS gets here," he remarked.

She gave him a brief grateful look. "Okay. Shall we take a look then?"

They pushed their way through the gathering crowds, Joe striding ahead, waving his arms and shouting, "Police, make way."

Someone said, "It's the Lady Inspector," and a speculative murmur rippled through the ranks.

Joe used the heightened interest to stage manage things a little. "Just move back folks, let the Inspector breathe. Shame it's necessary."

This raised a laugh and the crowd fell back good-naturedly. Amanda ducked under the tape and gingerly approached a pile of green plastic rubbish bags. When the smell hit her it was like walking into an iron wall. Gagging, she stopped dead and covered her face with the large handkerchief Meryl had sent for her. She then skirted the bags in small measured paces, attempting to see what was there without disturbing the site. A gull swooped on her, obviously bothered at the idea of competition for whatever delicacy lay beneath the plastic.

"I can see a hand," she told Joe. It was caked in filth, barely discernible, and there was something else. "Joe, it's another hand. Another *right* hand."

They looked at each other.

"Number four," she said grimly.

Beyond the cordon a voice lifted above the crowd, "It's a body!"

Amanda scanned the gawking mob. The uniform cops were keeping them back but God only knew what evidence they could be trampling beyond the immediate boundaries of the site. She shook the dust from her handkerchief and returned it to her face. The sun was climbing fast. Christ it was hot. Too hot to live.

"We need to clear this area, Joe," she said. "Call the station. Tell them to get some numbers down here. And tell Harry to close the dump. I don't care what the goddamn Council says."

A short, ginger-haired man with huge perspiration rings around his armpits broke through to the front of the throng. "Rodney Innes. Radio New Zealand News." He waved a microphone towards Amanda. "Inspector Valentine. Has the Garbage Dump Killer struck again?"

The Garbage Dump Killer. The crowd responded with a buzz of excitement.

"We have no comment to make at this stage," Amanda said tonelessly. She felt like picking up something gross and throwing it at him. From the time the first remains had been discovered at the dump twelve weeks ago, the press had been working themselves into a feeding frenzy over the case.

Joe was peering down into the mound of bags. "Definitely looks like two right hands to me."

"Did you say two right hands?" the reporter badgered. "That's two bodies, huh?"

"Stick it, buddy," Joe muttered.

The reporter promptly started blathering into his mike. "Police have this morning uncovered what appears to be a mass grave at the city garbage dump ..."

A mass grave. That really got the crowd going. They pressed forward, eyes glittering with a repulsive combination of horror and intrigue.

Amanda lost her temper. "Would you get these morons out of here!" she hissed at Joe.

Even as she said it, she could hear sirens and a convoy of blue and white cars appearing at the crest of the tip face. Blue lights flashing, they proceeded down the gravel road like a scene out of *Mad Max.* As the public were marveling at this spectacle, something else caught their attention and all heads swiveled upward like a wave.

Amanda heard the beat of chopper blades and, shielding her eyes, she looked up too. A Television New Zealand helicopter swooped low, raising a huge dust storm, then it simply hung there as though painted against the hazy sky.

"What the hell ..." Joe cursed.

The crowd became a sea of confusion as everyone attempted to escape the whirlwinds of stinging grit. One section of the tape gave way as a swell of people were crushed against it. The smell hit them and they fell back in disarray. A fat man in pink baggies threw up on a woman's feet. She started screaming at him. Her glasses fell off. Someone else trod on them.

Amanda closed her eyes against the dust, the

filth, the whole sickening spectacle. This can't be real, she told herself. In a minute, she would wake up alone in some verdant glade, stretched out on the cool, mossy bank of a bubbling stream, the scent of jasmine in the air, a benevolent sun kissing her flesh . . .

"Valentine," said a voice beside her, and Amanda opened her eyes to find her nightmare had just taken a turn for the worse.

A pair of watery blue eyes looked her up and down and Detective Inspector Special Duties, Robert B. Welch, announced in his schoolmaster voice, "Looks like things have got way out of hand here, Valentine . . . no crowd control, unauthorized media coverage . . ." His thin mouth twitched with disapproval.

Amanda eyed him warily. Bob Welch was a tall man whose neck and shoulders seemed too big for his head. There was something about him which always struck her as unkempt. It seemed an unfair judgment given the obvious care he took with his appearance. Invariably Welch was immaculately dressed, his thin reddish hair oiled flat, his pitted face brutally clean shaven. He stooped, as very tall people often did; a legacy of their teasing at school, she supposed. Bob Welch would have been the kind of teenager who got sand kicked in his face. No, it wasn't his looks. It was his smell. Stale. The faint clinging odor of used linen and cigarette smoke.

Amanda met his moist eyes and was ashamed to feel grateful for the fetid surroundings. At least while they were wading about in a sea of rotting garbage, she was in no danger of noticing that odd Bob Welch smell.

To her astonishment, Welch lit a cigarette and dragged deeply. Exhaling in her direction, he drawled, "Yep. Looks like you need all the help you can get. So let's have a look at this body, then."

Amanda stood where she was. "The body is almost entirely buried in rubbish and we're still waiting for McDougall to get here."

Welch looked impatient, mouthed something that was drowned in the roar of chopper blades. A few yards away the TVNZ helicopter was attempting to land. People were fleeing in all directions, most of them, thankfully, escaping to their cars.

Amanda waved Joe over and, pointing at the helicopter, shouted above the din, "Tell those assholes to get out of here. There's nothing for them to see, and they're destroying an evidence site. For God's sake. This kind of media circus is the worst thing that can happen in a serial killer case —"

"Serial killer," Bob Welch said dismissively. "You Americans have got serial killers on the brain. Any excuse for publicity . . ."

Amanda told herself to let it go. Bob Welch wasn't the enemy. He was just an old-fashioned cop who had a problem with women . . . and foreigners. And no doubt queers, solo mums, and black people . . . especially those in well-paid jobs. She didn't have to like him, she only had to work with him.

"Amanda." Joe's hand rested heavily on her shoulder.

She spun around. "What?"

She was looking straight into a TV camera. A half-dressed woman emerged from the crew and moved toward her.

"Is it true that you're nowhere near making an

arrest for the Garbage Dump Killings, Inspector Valentine?" Debby Daley chirped.

As Amanda stared, Joe broke in with a stock reply. "This is strictly police business. We are unable to comment at this time. Now if you don't mind, we have a job to do."

Debby circled them, a fine lace handkerchief cupped to her nose. "I understand you're dealing with a mass grave here, Inspector . . ."

Amanda lifted jaded eyes. In another life she would have said go screw yourself. Where did the press get off legitimizing their indecent curiosity, their exploitative filming, by deeming it news?

Inexplicably, Debby's expression altered. Expert smile fading, she lowered her microphone and started to speak, when there was a scream.

The TV crew clamored for angles. Amanda turned and her jaw dropped.

Bob Welch was perched on the mound of rubbish bags in a gamehunter's pose, a silly grin on his face.

"Oh my God." Debby swayed.

Amanda started laughing loudly, hysterically. Only the joke was on her.

At Bob Welch's feet was the naked body of a woman.

It was a plastic mannequin.

Madam was waiting in the driveway as Amanda pulled in. Amanda opened the car door automatically and the little tabby climbed inside and settled on her knee for the drive into the garage.

She'd ruined that cat, Kate had told her. Once

you let them take certain liberties, you couldn't stop them. They were worse than children.

Bleakly, she trudged up the internal stairwell into her sitting room and collapsed on the sofa. The afternoon sun was spilling in her windows, the room was hot and airless, her body ached and her eyelids felt like sandpaper. For a moment she sat cupping her forehead in her filthy hands, then she dragged herself into the bathroom and showered gratefully.

She felt exhausted, overwhelmed. She dispatched a message to the Garbage Dump Killer: *A curse on you.* No doubt the bastard would watch the news tonight, have a good laugh. He wouldn't be the only one.

She toweled herself mechanically, picked up Madam and slunk into her bed. Stroking the little cat and lulled by its contented purring, she drifted into merciful sleep, only to awaken almost immediately with a hideous jolt.

The doorbell. Amanda felt like crying. "Go away," she cursed. It rang again. This time she got up, stumbled to the door and leaning against the wall, flung it open.

"Hi there." It was Debby Daley, bursting out of a tight little polka-dot sundress.

Automatically Amanda glanced past her for the camera crew. There was just a white BMW convertible with the roof down. "What do you want?" she demanded.

Debby pushed her long tresses back as if she practiced doing it every morning in the mirror. Trust a blonde, Amanda thought.

"Can I come in?" she asked in a little-girl voice.

"No." Amanda started to close the door.

Debby's foot prevented her. "Please."

"Take your foot out of my door," Amanda said coldly.

Debby instantly retracted her pink sling-back. "I'm sorry. Please, Amanda ... Inspector ... It's important."

"I have nothing more to say."

"It's not about the Garbage Dump Killer," Debby insisted. "Honestly. It will only take five minutes ..." Catching Amanda's hesitation, she capitalized on it, adding, "I have some information for you."

Information. The irresistible currency of detective work. With a quick reckless glance at Debby's cleavage, Amanda shrugged. "Okay. Five minutes." The day couldn't get any worse.

She led Debby into the sitting room, turned on the ceiling fan and offered her a drink.

"Perrier, thanks."

"I don't buy French mineral water. Maybe I'll reconsider when they stop exploding their nuclear bombs on our back doorstep."

Debby's eyes widened and her red impeccable mouth parted. Amanda dragged her attention from its distracting fullness, the glimpse of pearly teeth, the dimples that played at its corners. "Then I'll have what you're having," Debby said breathlessly.

Amanda handed her a double Scotch, sat down at the opposite end of the sofa and waited for the predictable gasping and choking.

But Debby sipped the drink with demure panache. "Thank you for seeing me," she said unblinkingly. "First I just want to say I'm sorry about this afternoon."

Sorry. Amanda toyed with the word. "I'm sure

you are," she said cynically. "There wasn't much in it for you, was there? Twenty mannequins in a mass grave . . ." She gave a short, harsh laugh. Cheap shot, but who cared?

"I was worried about you." Debby lowered her empty glass to the coffee table and clasped her hands in her lap like a convent girl. "You looked so tired and down. It must have been so frustrating for you . . . I know you've been on this case for ages." She sought out Amanda's eyes. "I wondered if there was anything I could do to help. Like maybe fix you a meal or something. I mean you live alone, don't you? That woman yesterday . . ."

Amanda sat very still, met those remarkable aquamarine eyes and wondered what the hell Debby Daley was up to. She stated the obvious. "I don't think you've come here to cook me dinner."

Debby's mouth drooped. "What do you mean?"

"I mean you're a reporter, Debby." Amanda lounged back into the cushions and subjected the blonde to her most interrogative stare. "You're here because you want something. You say you have some information for me. How about coming to the point so I can go back to bed and get some sleep."

Debby raised a fine-boned hand to her mouth. "I woke you. I'm so sorry."

Amanda yawned pointedly.

"Well, there was something," her guest confessed in a rush. "I know you'll think this is a cheek, but well, I came to ask for your help."

Amanda stiffened. "My help?"

"It's kind of complicated. You see, I'm working on this story. Serious news." She paused significantly.

"I've found out about a crime and I want to discuss it with you."

"Go on." Maybe it was a theft ... someone had stolen Debby's brain.

"If you're willing, we could meet to discuss it."

"Why not tell me now?"

"It's a long story," Debby said quickly. "And I have to get to the studio. I just wanted to see if you were ... interested."

Interested? Amanda's nerves prickled. "I might be," she said cautiously. "Can you be more specific?"

"How about we talk over dinner. My place tomorrow?"

Common sense dictated she decline. But saying no to sexy women had never been one of Amanda's major strengths, brains or no brains. Besides she was curious, a little flattered. Who knows; maybe Debby was harboring an autographed publicity photo of the Garbage Dump Killer. "Sure," she said. "Why not?"

She got the address and walked Debby to the door.

Poised on the steps, Debby moistened her lips, touched Amanda's arm, and said huskily, "You won't regret it, Amanda. I promise."

CHAPTER FIVE

They were supposed to be building a new Central Police Station in Wellington, but in the meantime everyone was crowded into a ramshackle turn-of-the-century building with tiny grilled windows and dank stairwells.

They wouldn't tolerate it in Auckland, Wellington cops muttered in respect of their northern counterparts. Auckland was cop paradise, Sydney for beginners. Plenty of staff, plenty of perks and a huge voting population. When Auckland asked, central government sat up and took notice. When

Wellington asked they were told to be reasonable. Didn't they have the best clearance rate in New Zealand? Didn't they have a law-abiding population? Didn't they have it easy compared to Auckland cops?

Amanda's office was a cut above most. That was because she'd painted it herself a few weeks back. Instead of enduring flaking canary-tinted concrete, she now got to rejoice in the hedonism of pale cream with olive trim. She'd done the carpet as well, lifting the coarse rattan and laying a dark green square that used to occupy her spare room at home.

Joe was waiting there when she came on duty. He grinned. "You cleaned up okay."

Amanda dumped her briefcase on her desk and took the armchair beside his. "Two showers and I've still got crap in my ears," she grumbled. "How long did you stay down there?"

"Till we found what was smelling so godawful."

"What was it?"

"A ham," Joe said wryly. "Inside one of those muslin bags."

"Someone dumped the Christmas ham?"

"Jewish people won it in a raffle maybe. I never smelt anything like it . . . and the maggots!"

"Rotting flesh," Amanda said grimly. "Makes you think about cremation, doesn't it?"

"You get to see Jezebel?"

"They rang last night to say she's come 'round, so I'll interview her today."

"I want to bring Hippolyte in. The guy knows something."

"We've been over that, Joe. Besides, you talked to Zanette. His alibi checks out."

"You wanna catch the bastards or not?"

49

Amanda sighed deeply and met Joe's mellow brown eyes with a weary expression. "Maybe I'm losing it."

"You been putting in a lot of hours on the Garbage Dump Killer."

"I'm paid to."

"The force pays you, it don't own you, kid."

Amanda smiled wanly. "I guess I'm just having a confidence crisis, Joe. I've been on that case for twelve weeks. I've got twenty detectives on the job. The Commissioner is on the phone every day wanting results and we're nowhere." She hunched forward, resting her elbows on her knees. "Now some asshole tries to kill Jezebel, and they were decent enough to leave the weapon at the scene. But nobody knows anything —"

"I found her little black book," Joe broke in. "Real interesting."

Amanda threw him a jaundiced look. "Surprise me."

He passed her a list. "These are the guys with the most to hide."

Amanda flicked down the names. Politicians, city councilors, top unionists, half the local business round table. Lots of decent family men. Lots of wives who didn't know they were AIDS risks.

"Check them out, will you, Joe? Play it down ... we've had a complaint from one of her clients ... Anyone else had any problems?"

Joe snorted. "I'd say most of these jerks have got a problem."

Amanda refrained from getting into an ideological discussion and instead tossed Ricky Hippolyte's file across to him. "Read and digest," she said. "Start with his 'eighty-eight statement."

Joe leafed through, looked up with knitted brows, then turned the pages over one by one. "What statement? There's nothing here ..."

"Imagine that," Amanda drawled. "Surely we haven't gone and misfiled a statement which could implicate someone in the Force."

Joe stared at her.

There was a knock. Bob Welch poked his head around the door, saw her talking to Joe, and butted in anyway. "You got a minute, Valentine?"

Exchanging a look with Amanda, Joe got to his feet. As he left he muttered, "Shit."

Welch lowered himself into the chair Joe had just vacated and stretched his legs out in front of him.

Amanda tried not to notice the smell. He must have washed off the garbage dump, she thought distractedly. Maybe he used some kind of weird soap. Something that smelled ... stale.

He was speaking. She forced herself to concentrate.

"So the Chief tells me you're starting over there tomorrow," he droned.

Amanda stared at him blankly. "Where was that, Bob?"

"The Mayor's Office." He said it with a slight curl of the lips.

"The Mayor's Office?" Amanda repeated. What was the guy on about?

"The Chief mentioned you've been under a lot of stress and you being a female, with all the usual female ... er, *things* ..." He rambled on about the trouble with having females in key positions, they were so unreliable, them and their *female problems* . . .

Finally Amanda intruded on this compelling monologue. "Bob, what exactly are you getting at? You think the reason we haven't caught the Garbage Dump Killer is that I get a monthly period?"

A flush crept up Bob Welch's neck. Patting his lank hair down with a very large hand, he got to his feet. "I'll be honest with you, Valentine. I think Homicide is a man's province."

There was a certain logic to that, Amanda thought with bitter irony. Most killers were men, after all. Maybe it was only fair that men should be responsible for cleaning up after the horrors wrought by their gender, for bringing the perpetrators to justice. What did she get out of it? *Revenge*, her subconscious responded instantly. *It's my job*, she told herself and rose to her feet.

Welch was examining her office disdainfully. "Take this," he declared. "No *man* would sacrifice crucial hours in the course of a major inquiry to dolly up his office."

Amanda chose to ignore the obvious baiting. "I'm sure you've got things to do, Bob," she said, moving toward the door.

For a moment Welch didn't budge. Then he glanced down at her, pulled a packet of cigarettes from his pocket and took his time lighting up. Exhaling into her office, he stalked off.

* * * * *

52

Chief Inspector Bailey was a solid, good-humored man whose placid features were dominated by a pair of the most sharply intelligent brown eyes Amanda had ever seen. Those eyes were regarding her right now with laconic indulgence.

"I gather Welch has taken it upon himself to brief you," he said.

Amanda shook her head. "Not entirely, sir. Perhaps if you could explain . . ."

"Of course." He paused, tapping out his pipe. "As you are probably aware the City Council is about to invest in a new security system. Mayor Perkins has personally requested we assess their situation and make a few recommendations."

"A security system." Amanda gaped. "You mean alarms and guards and the like?"

"That included," the Chief said. "But I understand the Mayor is more concerned about documentation security. You might recall that budget deficit last year. Three million dollars unaccounted for."

"Looks pretty bad coming up to election time," Amanda observed.

"Indeed. I think the Mayor is rather hoping you might turn up a little information about the whereabouts of those funds."

Amanda frowned. "What about the Serious Fraud Squad?" The Department already had a squad of neatly manicured undercover boys who knew all about white-collar crime. "This is their area, sir, not mine."

"The Squad carried out an investigation into that

deficit last year, Valentine. I believe they attributed it all to misfiled accounting records and keying errors."

Amanda contemplated three million missing dollars and a lot of negative press for Mayor Perkins. Convenient ... for someone. She met the Chief's eyes squarely. "Who else is in the election race?"

"The Mayor's standing again. And there's the usual mob, that Hospital Board woman and a handful of greenies. Wilson, the deputy, is the main contender."

"What do we know about him?"

"He's in dog food. I believe the others are vegetarian." He toyed unenthusiastically with his pipe. "They don't inspire confidence, Valentine."

Amanda accepted his nugget unblinkingly. "So this is really about making Harvey Perkins look rosy so he can hang onto the Mayoralty for another term?"

With a faraway look, the Chief started to refill his pipe. "Let's just say what's good for Harvey is good for the city. I'll be frank with you, Valentine. You're a high-profile detective. In assigning you, and not some junior, we're letting the Mayor know he's important."

In other words, if they played their cards right, Harvey Perkins would screw Central Government for a bigger Police Department budget. Maybe they would get their new station sooner.

"I see," Amanda said with a trace of bitterness. So much for leaving politics behind when she'd left NYPD.

"Naturally I don't expect you to maintain your

present caseload in addition to this assignment ..."
the Chief went on, cupping his pipe in one hand.

As she listened, Amanda was gripped by a chill
suspicion. Could it be possible that the Chief was
looking for reasons to take her off the Garbage
Dump case? "Sir," she broke in quickly, "I hope this
has nothing to do with the performance of Big Mack.
I know we don't have a prime suspect yet, but we're
building a picture of his modus operandi. I know
he's going to strike again soon. He's only waiting for
the temperature to drop."

The Chief eyed her quizzically.

"It's the heatwave," she explained. "Imagine
hacking up a corpse in this weather. Underneath it
all, I think our man is a more meticulous
personality than we first assumed. His behavior
suggests expedience as well as kicks. He shows an
organized pattern."

The Chief smiled briefly, then carried on as if he
hadn't heard her. "More experienced men than you
have developed stress-related illnesses during this
type of inquiry, Valentine."

His words jolted her. Surely the Chief didn't
subscribe to Bob Welch's "delicate womanhood"
theories as well. "I have my own ways of dealing
with stress." She tried not to sound defensive. "I
think they're effective."

The Chief examined her thoughtfully. "I'm sure
they are. However, we can't afford to put your
health at risk. Besides, Welch has offered to take
over the investigation. I think it's time we gave him
an opportunity to show us what he's made of ..."

"Sir, I object!" Amanda was shaking. How could
the Chief even consider handing the case over to

Bob Welch? "I think you're making a big mistake . . ."

She fell silent at the Chief's warning stare. "Why do you say that, Valentine?" His voice was dangerously soft.

She shook her head. She had no real basis on which to found her doubts about Bob Welch's professional competence. No self-respecting cop permitted personal feelings to cloud his or her judgment. Fighting to keep her voice steady, she played the best card she had. "Sir, I'm the only detective in New Zealand with any experience investigating repeat homicide. I solved the Sauna Strangler case in nine weeks and back home I was on two task forces using NCAVC techniques. We had top profilers working with us . . ."

The Chief treated her to a piercing look. "I'm familiar with your background, Valentine. Why do you think I chose you to lead this inquiry rather than one of our more experienced homicide detectives?"

The message was clear. The Chief had gone out on a limb and now Amanda had to deliver. "I'll get him, sir," she promised.

"I hope so. Meantime, Welch will take over the rest of your caseload."

Relief washed the panic from Amanda's limbs. Suppressing a foolish urge to thank him profusely, she reiterated, "We *are* making progress."

"Pity about the media hype over those dummies."

Amanda looked heavenward. "Sir, I . . ."

The Chief lit his pipe. It was his signal that the discussion was closed. She got to her feet.

"One more thing, Valentine," he added as she was leaving the office. "Do yourself a favor and get the press off your tail. The Commissioner mentioned it."

CHAPTER SIX

Fat chance, Amanda thought as she pulled up outside Debby Daley's. The place was a cute turn-of-the-century villa in Thorndon. It was surrounded by numerous rinky-dink companions in a short stretch of road that looked like the Liberals' Last Stand. Every house had Neighborhood Watch stickers on its stained glass bow windows, every minute front yard boasted olde-worlde rose bushes and most of the cars in the Residents Only parking were Citroens and MGs with Greenpeace bumper stickers. Most of the sound systems inside the quaint cottages were worth more than the cars, Amanda guessed. Tonight most of them were playing Tracy Chapman.

The evening was thick and airless, the sun slithering slowly behind the hills. Amanda locked the Toyota and wriggled inside her sweaty clothes. You wouldn't think she'd showered less than an hour ago.

Pushing her hair off her face, she banged on Debby's door and lurched back as it was instantly opened.

"Amanda! Come on in." Debby was acting as if Father Christmas had just arrived.

She showed Amanda into a sitting room that Amanda found completely unexpected. The stereo was playing Vivaldi. The curtains were faded and rosy, the sofa was soft and welcoming, and the walls were covered in upscale real art that made Amanda drool. The whole place was tranquil and well worn, downright homey in fact, and it smelled of Debby's perfume Obsession.

"What can I get you?" Debby was over in one corner of the room opening a small bar behind a fold-out bookcase.

"Just water, thanks." Amanda studied her covertly as the drinks were poured.

Debby was sewn into another cocktail get-up; this time an off-the-shoulder mini-dress in pink silk. Her hair was loose and looked like a shampoo commercial, long sparkly earrings dangling against the blonde. She had a sensational body. There was no getting away from it. She was medium height, but her legs were long and shapely, her breasts were full and her backside deserved an essay all its own.

She handed Amanda her drink and perched on

the arm of the couch, gazing across her glass with rapt blue-green eyes. "You know," she said huskily, "you're not too bad yourself, Amanda."

Conscious she had started to blush, Amanda peered down at her drink and willed her pulse to slow down. "I'm sorry if I was staring. Your, er . . . dress is quite fantastic."

"I have a wardrobe with my show," Debby explained. "One of my main functions is to be a clotheshorse, you see."

"Fashion labels give you the stuff so you'll model it on the show?"

"That's right. And I get to keep everything. That's in my contract."

"What were you doing before you got the show?"

"I lived in Auckland. I was modeling for a while, then I finished my journalist training and got a job in the newsroom."

"Then you got 'discovered?' "

Debby shook her head. "I wrote the first few shows myself, filmed them on the cheap and offered them to the station."

Amanda felt her interest level leap a notch or two. "So how do you choose your subjects?"

"I talk to my viewers, find out who they're interested in, and I ask my guests exactly the questions the viewers would."

"Is that how you chose me?"

"Oh, I've been watching you for a while, Inspector," Debby's tone was teasing. "You're news. You just got a royal decoration, you're American, people are amazed that a woman like you can also be a tough cop . . ."

A woman like her. What did that mean? "I'm not sure whether to be flattered by that —"

"Oh, you should be," Debby told her dead-pan. "I only choose talent for my show. Just being famous or rich isn't enough. I want to interview special people. People who make the world work better."

Mediaspeak. Feeling squeamish, Amanda followed Debby into the dining room.

The meal was wonderful. Gazpacho followed by a smoked salmon souffle and salad, with double-dipped profiteroles to finish. Debby obviously had top-dollar catering, probably claimed it as a job expense.

She was prattling on in her soft, girly voice. Amanda stifled a hiccup and forced herself to listen. Debby seemed to be talking about her childhood in Singapore. Evidently her father had been stationed there in the Air Force.

Amanda's hands went clammy straight away. Had things got that personal already or was Debby just one of those people who told their life stories instead of talking about the weather?

She had a pleasing mid-Atlantic accent. No doubt she'd been trained out of the Kiwi twang by some PR firm. She kept seeking out Amanda's eyes and pausing after each sentence as though waiting for some unspoken cue. Amanda studied her mouth. It was very full and her lipstick appeared to have survived the meal intact. Maybe she'd reapplied it in the kitchen between courses ...

Debby caught her staring, and smiled a little too warmly. "So how come you're working in New Zealand?"

Reminding herself that she was a seasoned

professional, Amanda uneasily loosened the top button of her shirt. "My Dad is a Kiwi. He came back here after he and Mom were divorced. At the time I was at a bit of a loose end." She kept her voice as bland as she could. A loose end ... that was one way of putting it. "Because of Dad, I've got dual citizenship, so I wrote to a couple of the Universities out here. Victoria offered me a tutoring job while I finished my PhD."

"And then you joined the police."

"Yes."

It hadn't been quite that simple. She'd had no intention of joining the police when she moved to New Zealand. She was finished with being a cop, forever.

She'd moved into a sunny upstairs flat in an old Mount Victoria house. Her neighborhood was inner city and gentrified, teeming with yuppies and women living alone. It was walking distance from Wellington's version of Chinatown and it reminded Amanda vaguely of San Francisco and happier times.

The place had been terrorized by a knife-wielding rapist for nearly a year. But that wasn't Amanda's problem. She was there to finish her thesis and make the most of life in the slow lane.

It was 3:00 AM and Amanda had been lying awake, as she often did, haunted by Kelly's face, cold and waxen, a lavender ribbon around her black curls, her laughing eyes closed forever.

At first she'd ignored the soft scrape, the rattle, a thud. Then she heard what sounded like a choked scream. Adrenalin pumping, she'd thrown on her sneakers, dusted off her trusty .357 and slipped noiselessly out her door. Skirting the level below, she noticed the wash-house window open and the distinct impression of a man's foot in the damp earth beneath it. Amanda eased herself inside and crept along an unlit passageway.

The rapist had already tied up and gagged her neighbor, a middle-aged widow, and was busy telling her how he planned to cut her throat with the large kitchen knife resting next to him on the bed if she made any noise.

He was a large man but not a skilled fighter, Amanda guessed in a split-second assessment. He was a little flabby, and over-confident enough to put down a weapon while he was tying up his victim. In other words, a pushover. Pity, she thought. She would have liked an excuse to take out a kneecap or two.

Almost forgetting she wasn't a cop, Amanda walked calmly into the room, tapped his shoulder, and sliding her gun against his ribs, told him he was under arrest.

Predictably, he reared back in a panic and threw up an arm to try and knock the gun aside. Amanda deflected the blow gracefully, kicked him twice in the kidneys, then, as he stooped in agony, clubbed him casually across the base of the neck. Once he was on the floor, she ordered him onto his stomach and informed him that if he moved he'd be eating brains. She located a stocking of her neighbor's and trussed him neatly, then turned her attention to Mrs. Lorraine Plimmer who, once ungagged, immediately urged her to kill the bastard.

"That would be murder, I'm afraid," Amanda informed the older woman while she was untying her.

"Then shoot off his balls."

Amanda shook her head. "Too obvious, Mrs. Plimmer. But I'm going to go and ring the police now. What say you punch and kick him some while I'm in the other room and we'll call that self-defense."

Not long after that, Amanda had found herself applying for a job in the Wellington CIB. Once a cop, always a cop, her Dad had said cheerfully.

"So you don't plan on going back to the States?" Debby was asking.

Amanda frowned slightly. "I honestly don't know, Debby. I love it here but I miss home too. My Mom's living in Saratoga now. That's a pretty little place near the mountains in New York State. I've visited her a couple of times but I haven't been back to the city."

Debby stared at her long and hard. "I feel that way about Singapore," she said huskily. "I miss it, but I hated the place too. I'm scared that if I ever go back all I'll feel is the hate."

Amanda gazed silently down at her hands. Then she made a show of looking at her watch. "It's late."

"You don't have to run off." Debby threw her a candid look. "We can stick to small talk if it makes you more comfortable."

Amanda lifted guilty eyes. So much for the impenetrable facade of the senior detective. "No, I should be going. Thanks for the meal."

"You don't have anyone at home to cook for you?"

"I'm not married if that's what you mean."

"That wasn't your flatmate then?"

"That was a friend."

"Nice," Debby said. "Friends who sleep over. I

guess in your line of work there's not much time for a private life." With a wistful expression she pushed her hair back behind her shoulders. These were almost in the same league as her backside, smooth, lightly tanned, unexpectedly muscular. Aerobics, Amanda decided.

"I imagine your life revolves pretty much around your work too," she observed a little stiltedly.

Debby nodded. "Sometimes the hours are really erratic."

"Like first thing Saturday mornings?"

"If that's the only time I can catch a subject."

"Do you make a habit of calling unannounced?"

Debby looked at her blankly.

"Like you did with me."

"You weren't expecting me?"

"Was I supposed to be?"

Debby frowned. "I arranged that time with one of your colleagues. Inspector Bob Welch. He said you were off duty but he would confirm with you. He said he knew you'd be fine about it."

Amanda was silent. What in God's name did Bob Welch think he was doing playing her press secretary? Obviously he'd forgotten to mention Debby Daley to her. Irritated, she said, "I guess he must have put something in my tray and it got buried."

"Gosh, I'm so sorry," Debby seemed genuinely embarrassed. She stretched out a hand and touched Amanda lightly on the knee. "I feel terrible about that. I just assumed you knew."

Amanda gazed at the hand on her knee. It was smooth-skinned, the fingers long and expressive. She tried not to imagine it sliding a little further. Debby was heterosexuality personified, she told herself, and she herself was a senior police officer. She cleared her throat, remembering she had originally come here for a reason. "What was it you wanted to see me about, Debby?"

Debby's hand flew to her mouth. "Silly me. I almost forgot." She moved a little further along the sofa, gazing into Amanda's eyes. "I need your help. I'm working on a serious news story." She emphasized the word serious. Amanda figured someone like Debby Daley would have to.

"How can I help?"

"I've discovered something dreadful."

You've got dandruff, Amanda thought uncharitably.

"It's to do with drugs," Debby said. "I met this guy at a party for the producer of *Kiwi Lifestyle.*"

"That show where rich people brag off to other rich people?"

Debby looked uncomfortable. "He was kind of hitting on me ..."

"That's legal." Amanda wished she would get to the punchline.

"I really want to do serious news," Debby repeated with a brave tremble. She was so close to Amanda their thighs were brushing. "This is big," she revealed breathlessly. "I'm certain of it. It's drugs, hard drugs. People are getting bribed."

Amanda's lips twitched.

"You don't think I'm serious." Debby sounded hurt.

Avoiding her eyes, Amanda said in her most reasonable tone, "What do you want from me,

Debby? You're talking about some kind of drug racket. You say people are getting bribed. Do you have any evidence?"

Debby shook her head miserably. "That guy I talked to ... he was drunk, showing off. Men always think I don't understand or I'll forget or something."

Amanda's eyes trailed over the woman beside her. Yes, she could believe that.

"He offered me drugs. All sorts — coke, hash, ecstasy."

Despite herself, Amanda's interest quickened. "You mean he was selling?"

"Oh, no," Debby dropped her voice. "He was giving it away."

Sure, Amanda thought. *Quid pro quo.* "What's the guy's name?"

"Chris Clarke."

"What else do you know about him?"

"Not much." Debby gave a faint shudder. "He's not exactly the kind of guy you feel drawn to."

"You gave him the brush-off?"

"He was a creep."

"Okay. So a creep offers you free drugs, presumably because he wants to sleep with you. What do you want me to do?"

Debby stared at her, a trace of disillusionment tugging the corners of her mouth down. "I guess I was hoping you could investigate him. Bust him and cut me in on the deal. I want to do a hard news story on white-collar drug dealers in Wellington."

"It's a great idea." Amanda found it within herself to offer a crumb of encouragement. "But narcotics is not my area, Debby. The best I can do is give you the name of someone on the Vice Squad —"

"I've been checking out this guy," Debby persisted. "It's weird. A lot of people know him — top people. But no one seems to know what he does for a living."

"Has anyone inferred he sells drugs?"

"Not exactly. But —"

"Look." Amanda sighed. "I can't spark off a narcotics inquiry on the strength of hearsay. We don't have the staff or the time. Get me something concrete on this guy Clarke and we can talk again. Okay?"

"Really? You'd do it?" Debby's eyes were bright and dark, her mouth deliciously curved. Her fingers trailed down Amanda's arm to her hand. "There must be something I can do for you in exchange ..."

Amanda's skin prickled. What sort of exchange did Debby have in mind? Steering her thoughts away from the obvious, she got hastily to her feet. Then an idea registered. "Actually, there is something," she said, congratulating herself on her presence of mind. "You can hold off running that interview."

"Hold off. Why?"

"I can't go into details. But what I can tell you is that the interview could jeopardize an important case I'm working on right now." Not to mention getting up the Commissioner's nose.

At once, Debby's gaze sharpened. "Is it the Garbage Dump Killer? Are you onto someone?"

"I'm not at liberty to comment on that, Debby.

All I'm asking is for you to hold up on the program."

"I'll try. But I don't control these things." Debby was on her feet also. "Surely you don't have to go already," she said softly. "I was hoping we could have some social time together. Forget about our jobs for a couple of hours."

Amanda read the entreaty in her face with suspicion. "Why?"

"Because I like you. I find you interesting."

The words hung in the air, suspended with Amanda's breathing. "I have to go, Debby. Maybe we could save it for another day."

"You think I'm a dumb blonde?"

Amanda started guiltily. "No. I don't."

"Then why won't you stay?" Debby rested a hand on her shoulder. "Is it because it would bother your friend?"

"My friend?" Amanda looked carefully blank. The hand on her shoulder felt very hot.

"The woman in the nightdress." Debby's face had lost all sign of limpid cuteness. Her eyes were suddenly knowing, her mouth full and sensual.

Time to leave, Amanda decided. Debby was coming on to her. It wasn't her imagination. She took a step back. "Thanks again for the meal, Debby. Remember what I said about your guy Clarke. Concrete facts."

"I'll do my best." Debby smiled, once more the talk-show hostess. She bent forward, brushed Amanda's cheek lightly with her lips. She waved cheerfully from her doorstep as Amanda let herself out the little picket gate.

* * * * *

It was midnight when she flicked on the lights in her kitchen. The place was stifling hot from being closed up all day. Amanda turned on the fan and tilted her face to it. She was flushed. The heat, of course.

The fridge beckoned and she approached automatically, peered inside for longer than necessary, closed it again. With a furtive glance at the cat door, she gravitated to the coffee machine and cooked up a double-strength brew. She could cut down tomorrow.

She slouched into the living room, cup in hand, and stretched out full length on the sofa. The coffee burned. She was taking it in careless gulps, your typical caffeine junkie. Somewhere in the back of her mind she was rolling her own skin-flick. Herself and Debby Daley, the pink mini-dress gone, those sleek limbs smooth and firm to the touch, Debby's hair spread all over the pillows, her eyes closed, her mouth soft.

Tossing aside the mail she'd extracted from her letterbox on the way in, Amanda grabbed the newspaper and foraged through the front pages. Plenty of low-minded political activity and sensationalist headlines, the kind of crap writing that passed for journalism. It was sufficient to drag her mind out of her pants and refresh her memory on the quality of the Fourth Estate for at least fifteen minutes.

After that she got morose. What kind of detective was she? A pushover, if the lissome Debby was anything to go by; a pushover with DYKE stamped on its forehead. Did Debby have that kind of radar or was she out to nail some hard evidence firsthand? What a tool. Give me the scoops or I'll hand them your career on a platter. What would Amanda say to that ... *Make my day, punk?*

She finished her coffee and peered regretfully at the residue in the bottom of her cup. She wanted another one. But she also wanted some sleep. She got up, paced restlessly into the kitchen, put the newspaper in the recycle bin and stacked her cup in the dishwasher.

Her eyes strayed past the phone. She hadn't listened to her messages and she didn't want to. With a loud sigh she pressed the play button.

Her mother. *Amanda, honey. You should see the sunsets here. Why don't you come over. I read all about Queen Elizabeth giving you a medal. Honey, I just want to share with you how proud I am of my little girl.*

The deli. *Were you serious about the sushi?*

Kate. *Hi, Amanda. I've left your spare key inside the washing machine. Good luck.* Great. Hey, thanks. Nothing like the personal touch.

Debby Daley. *Thanks for coming around, Amanda. I'll do what I can about the show. Can I see you again?*

Amanda poured herself another coffee and carried it into the bathroom. She peeled off her clothes and showered methodically for five minutes. Just enough time to wash off the soap.

Can I see you again? Translated: can we fuck?

Hello, New Zealand, this is Debby Daley and did you know our glamour cop is a dyke? I can prove it.

Maybe Debby normally acquired her unique

71

insights on her back. It added a whole new meaning to investigative journalism, Amanda mused. Was she really hinting she would trade sex for information?

Amanda played with the idea. Debby comes on to her. They go to the bedroom, make out for a while. Debby is panting, aroused. Amanda makes her squirm, beg ... Then she says they'd better stop because she never has sex in January. It's too hot ... That will teach you not to mess with lesbians, she gloats.

Ashamed, she crawled into bed. Maybe Debby wasn't straight at all. Maybe Debby just plain fancied her. Was that so improbable? She threw off her quilt and rolled onto her stomach, sharply conscious of a throbbing between her legs.

Maybe she just plain fancied Debby Daley, she thought miserably.

CHAPTER SEVEN

It was hot and musty in the Mayor's Office. Her first morning and the air conditioner wasn't working. Abandoned by the Goddess, Amanda thought glumly. She wished she could wander around in shorts with her shirt untucked like half the men she saw.

She'd been assigned a temporary desk in the Accounts Department, under the auspices of its Chief, Lillian Bennett, a woman she hadn't met yet. The place was barren of color and interest, its walls faded hospital yellow and the floor covered in pitted brown linoleum. A broken wall clock above the door said 5:30.

It had been that way for a year, said the dark-haired woman at the next desk. Her name was Margaret Kleist and the sign on her desk said Junior Accountant. She described herself as Lillian's slave and constantly glared toward the new oak door with Lillian's name on it. That morning she'd already kicked it several times in passing.

Amanda tried to imagine what sort of woman would inspire such loathing in her staff. "You don't get on with Lillian Bennett," she finally observed.

Margaret paused, her quick glance automatically ticking off the danger list. Lillian's office was empty, all doors were closed, no footsteps approaching. "Lillian hates me. I don't know why. She was nice to me for a couple of weeks, then she didn't bother any more."

"How long have you been here?"

"Two years."

"And you're unhappy?"

"I guess I am. It's not all Lillian's doing. It's the place too. It gets you down after a while. Everything is so inefficient. When I first got here I noticed all these stupid pointless procedures, like forms people fill out for reports no one uses any more and nit-picking reviews of petty expenditure when the big ones go straight through."

"And it's still the same?"

"Sure. I used to draw stuff to Lillian's attention. Suggest ways we could change things to save time and money. I even wrote it all in reports, but they never got past her of course. I think she just threw them in the bin. Management's prerogative."

Amanda concealed her disgust behind a neutral professionalism. "You know why I'm here?"

Margaret pointed at a memo on the noticeboard. "To examine security issues and evaluate the model for the new system."

All in a week, too. "That's right." She tried to sound enthusiastic. "Tell me, who would I talk to about internal audit?"

Margaret laughed. "At the moment no one really. There's a vacant position for internal auditor. We've been advertising for a year."

"No suitable applicants?"

"I'm not sure. At one stage there was a guy appointed but he changed his mind just before he was due to take up the position."

"Who's responsible for making that appointment?"

"Well, they get interviewed by a panel and Lillian's on that. Then they make a short list and those guys are interviewed by Mr. Wilson."

"Michael Wilson, the Deputy Mayor?"

Margaret nodded. "Then he makes a recommendation to the Town Clerk."

"And in the meantime no one is doing the auditing?"

"I offered to help, but Lillian said I was far too busy and she couldn't spare me."

Amanda glanced at the oak door. "Where is Lillian?"

Margaret shrugged. "At a meeting." She checked her watch. "It's morning tea time. Do you want to come up to the cafeteria? The food's atrocious but you could meet everyone."

And no doubt learn their theories on the Garbage Dump Killer too. "I'll hold on that one, thanks,

Margaret," Amanda said. "I'd better get some work done." She slid her fingers around the damp neck of her shirt and fantasized about an ice cold gin and tonic served beneath swaying palm trees by a nubile woman in a skimpy sarong, long blonde hair spilling across her naked shoulders. She removes the sarong and invites Amanda to come swimming. They cross hot, golden sand to the water's edge. Suddenly it's *From Here To Eternity* . . .

Amanda snapped guiltily to attention. Someone was asking her a question. It was a red-haired woman parked on the edge of her desk, nursing a thick file. Amanda noticed her fingernails with guilty fascination. They were at least an inch long and thickly coated in an apricot color which matched the suit she was wearing.

Dead fish eyes met hers and the woman dished out a barely thawed smile. "I'm Lillian Bennett. Welcome to my department, Inspector." It sounded as sincere as a fifties housewife saying, "Oh how super, only five cockroaches in the kitchen this morning."

Amanda thanked her.

"You're younger than I expected," Lillian said, coral lips pursed.

This was not a compliment, Amanda decided. She pushed her hair back and said apologetically, "I look younger than I really am, Ms. Bennett."

The tepid smile became glacial. "Do call me Lillian," said the well-preserved Chief Accountant.

She started leafing through the file she carried and again Amanda was transfixed by those nails. This time Lillian caught her staring. To Amanda's amazement she actually preened.

"I'll let you into a little secret." She dropped her

voice to a stage whisper. "They're fake." With a pitying expression, she glanced at Amanda's fingers. "Fabu-Nail. The clinic's only a block away. I'm sure they could do something for you."

"Thank you," Amanda whispered.

Lillian patted her hand. "I used to be a nail-biter, too." She uncrossed her stockinged legs and indicated her door. "Would you mind stepping into my office for a moment, Inspector?"

"Sure." Amanda quit feeling her nails for rough edges and followed Lillian through the big oak door.

Lillian's office paid particular homage to Laura Ashley. Tiny flowers galloped in all directions and a pink room freshener sat squarely on Lillian's desk, releasing a powdery ladies room scent. Holding down a sneeze, Amanda occupied a pastel armchair and studied Lillian Bennett.

The older woman seemed nervous all of a sudden, her pale eyes darting, her cheeks dull red beneath her peach blusher. "I'll come right to the point," she announced as if she were auditioning lines for daytime television. "I know why you're here and let me tell you I have no intention of walking out of this job just because Michael Wilson wants to replace me with one of the brethren. I've swum in shit to get this." Her hand traveled shakily around the busy decor.

"I'm sure you have," Amanda said, controlling her astonishment at this outburst.

"I don't know whose side you're on," Lillian continued in a similar vein, "but let me tell you I've kept records. In writing. And if I lose my job they're going straight to the press." She paused, evidently to let that sink in.

"Records?" Amanda ventured.

Lillian was unlocking a cabinet. She retrieved a thick file and slapped it down on her desk, stabbing it with a triumphant finger. "It's all here and I've made copies! I'm not going to sit back and be scapegoated for this! Just you try it!"

What the hell was she on about? "Lillian." Amanda sought refuge in a spot of lowest common denominator psychology. "You've done the right thing, bringing this to my attention."

The Chief Accountant scoured Amanda's face, her own revealing a mixture of emotions. Suspicion. Fear. Righteous indignation. Finally, relief appeared to triumph over paranoia, and glancing over her shoulder, she hissed, "It's Michael Wilson. He's after the Mayor's job, that snake in the grass. He told me to mind my own business or I might have none to mind!"

"What exactly has he asked you to keep quiet about?" Amanda asked delicately.

Lillian's lips twitched. Opening the file, she pulled out a mountain of paper slips and invoices. "It's all here. Read these and you'll see exactly what I'm talking about." She lifted the huge pile of papers and dumped them squarely in Amanda's lap. "Corruption," she declared. "It's a dirty business."

Staking out the Public Library was not how Amanda had envisaged spending her free time. Joe had called early in the afternoon to inform her he needed to sit with Meryl while she had a tooth extracted. Ricky Hippolyte was in the library and could Amanda watch him for a few minutes?

Amanda was holed up on the mezzanine floor. Sharing her table were a couple of students making a Gothic fashion statement and a drunk looking at sex manuals. Ten feet below, with his nose in a car handbook, was Hippolyte.

"People fucking," the drunk announced. "At it all the time."

No one paid any attention. "Fornication and adultery," he said louder. "Be damned, you sinners."

The students looked up. "Halitosis," said one to the other.

A man in a suit and a loud tie joined Ricky's table, and sat immersed in a marketing magazine.

The drunk staggered downstairs, leaving his book open at the section entitled *Foreplay Can Be Fun*. "Like yer tits," he crooned to the librarian.

"I'm going to ring the security guard," she said sternly.

The man in the loud tie approached the counter, leaving his magazine on the table. "I'll get rid of him," he volunteered.

The librarian fluttered, put the phone down.

"Take yer hands off me, yer homo," shouted the drunk.

Along with everyone else in the room, Ricky Hippolyte watched the suit hustle the bum outdoors. Moments later, he closed his book and idly picked up the magazine the suit had left behind.

There was something inside it. An envelope. Ricky pocketed it and walked out. On his way he left a tip on the counter for the astonished librarian.

Amanda followed him, doggedly trying to recall the face of the man in the suit. He was mid-thirties, medium-built, brown haired, clean shaven; but for the tie, eminently forgettable. And he had passed an envelope to Ricky Hippolyte.

Ricky was sauntering along Cuba Street. Amanda knew where he was headed. The Exotique A Go-Go Club. It was a safe bet to assume he'd be there the rest of the day. What was in the envelope? Money? Product?

Amanda watched him turn onto Vivian, head for the dim entrance to the club and climb the grimy stairs. Then she called Joe.

"The Library was a drop. He's at the Exotique now and he's carrying an envelope. He'll dump it if he sees me up there."

"Okay. I'll be there in ten minutes. You see his contact?"

"Yeah, some yuppie type. Drew a blank with me."

"So we'll pick up Hippolyte with the goods on board and bring him in for a little chat."

"Not yet," Amanda said. She felt Joe's sigh more than she heard it. "I'm more interested in the suit. Punks like Hippolyte don't have the brains to operate alone. The guy's a bit player in someone else's script and this time we've got a crack at the bastards."

Joe sounded pained. "We could be pissing around on this one for months with nothing to show for it."

"We won't be."

"What makes you so bloody certain?"

Amanda chewed her top lip thoughtfully. "A feeling," she said. "Same as the Chan case."

"Christ, Amanda. You wanna keep that kinda

stuff to yourself, kid. That was creepy that Chan business. Jesus Christ." He paused, chewing noises came over the phone, then he mumbled, "Maybe he knows sweet FA about Jezebel, but you wanna find out what really happened in 'eighty-eight, let's bring him in."

Amanda deliberated for a long moment. It had to be possible to question Hippolyte without scaring off the big boys. She wondered how Jezebel was tangled up in all of this. Maybe she wasn't. "Okay, pick him up," she said flatly. "But let's keep it to ourselves."

CHAPTER EIGHT

En route to the Station, Amanda stopped by the hospital. "I brought you something, Jezebel."

The aging transvestite raised her painted eyebrows. "For me!" She seized the gift-wrapped parcel in her bandaged hands and shook it. "Well, it ain't chocolates," she pronounced and handed it back. "You open it, lovie."

Amanda discarded the silvery wrapping and lifted the lid.

Jezebel squealed. "Oh, you shouldn't have." She tipped out a spangled G-string and matching garter.

"Paris, too." She examined the label. "That's what I like about you, doll. You got style. None of your cheap nylon."

Amanda smiled. "Are they treating you properly?"

"The nurses are real sweet even though they're trying to poison me with that godawful food."

"And the doctors?"

"You mean the one who looks like he got a cucumber stuck up there."

Amanda covered her mouth discreetly. "Yes, that one in particular."

"Oh, that boy's got some problems, hasn't he? You can only feel sorry for the closety types, my dear. They're so," she hunted for a word then lowered her voice, "tense."

Amanda grinned. "I know just what you mean. Any progress remembering the attack?"

Jezebel shook her bandaged head. "It's like it never happened. I don't even remember waking up that day, sweet girl. I could have died and I wouldn't even have noticed! Perhaps that's the way the Lord Jesus means for us to pass on over. In a state of bliss." She closed her blackened eyes and sighed profoundly.

"Your flat was wrecked. Do you remember that?"

Jezebel shook her head sadly. "Louella, my friend at the Perfumed Palazzo, she's been cleaning up in there and got the insurance man in. She told me all about it."

"Can you think of any reason someone might have done this to you, Jezebel, anything at all?"

At that Jezebel laughed raucously. "Why I can think of hundreds, dear, simply hundreds!"

"Like blackmail maybe?"

Jezebel averted her eyes.

Amanda lifted one of Jezebel's damaged hands. "Is that why someone did this? Is that why they tried to kill you?"

"Kill me." Jezebel slumped back into her pillows. Her face was at once tired and overwhelmingly sad. A mottled tapestry of cuts and bruises, it was puckered across her nose and around her mouth where the black sutures held it together. A tear trickled down her pitted cheek and dispersed across a patch of stray stubble. "I don't know, doll." She shook her head wearily. "No one hates me that bad. I'm not important enough to hate that bad."

Amanda slid back in the wobbly visitor's chair and put her feet up on the bed. "Somebody thinks you are," she said quietly. "Tell me about Ricky Hippolyte."

Jezebel studied the bedspread. "What about him?"

"Did you talk to him any time before it happened? In the past few months, say."

"Sure, doll. I said hello. He bought me a drink. Ricky's been buying everyone a drink. Girls say he's doin real well."

"Dealing?"

Jezebel shook her head emphatically. "No."

"What then?"

Jezebel shrugged. "Go talk to the boy."

Amanda tried again. "Did Ricky do it?"

"That weed. I doubt it."

"Jezebel," she began more sternly. A restraining hand touched her elbow.

"I'm sorry, Inspector, Jezebel needs to rest now."

Amanda looked up past a profound bosom to a pair of cool green eyes. She offered her most winning smile. The eyes flicked away, returned blatantly speculative.

"I'll only be five more minutes."

"No, you won't," the nurse said sweetly. "We have our rules, Inspector." She looked Amanda up and down with an expression of refined carnality.

"It's true, lovie," Jezebel said. "They're very big on discipline here. Makes a girl feel right at home."

Amanda swung her feet off the bed and stood up, feeling the nurse's appreciative gaze slide down her body again. "Looks like I'm outta here." She touched Jezebel's shoulder lightly. "If you think of anything, tell them to get hold of me."

"Sure, doll." Jezebel smiled, displaying a set of poorly fitting hospital issue dentures. "And thanks for the panties. You're an angel."

She blew kisses as Amanda walked out. Amanda knew there was something she wasn't saying.

It bugged her all the way to the Station. Blackmail. It had to be the explanation. Jezebel had no jealous pimp or lover. She didn't drink or do drugs. Her family accepted her as she was. Her neighbors liked her. Her landlord said she paid on time and what she had under her frock was none of his business and there was worse lowlife in this world and God only knew how he was ever going to get her place fixed up before she got out of the hospital.

Amanda had been over that phone call a thousand times. *Got me some rough trade ... they know I'm in here.* They. Rough trade — a john with a violence problem? A working stiff?

Joe had phoned every john in Jezebel's little black book and drawn a blank. Businessmen, politicians, lawyers. Nice class of customer. No, they'd never heard of a person called Jezebel and no, they weren't being blackmailed, thank you very much.

Hippo. Ricky Hippolyte. What was the connection? Was Jezebel blackmailing him? If she was, it certainly wouldn't be over the usual B & D photos. The only metal in Ricky's life was the likes of Twisted Sister.

The instant Amanda stepped into the inquiry center, an elegant dark-haired man pounced on her with an air of carefully contained excitement.

At a glance, Detective Senior Sergeant Austin Shaw appeared better suited to the pages of *GQ* than the rigors of homicide investigation. But Amanda had never met a more committed and meticulous cop. Shaw took every case personally, viewed every criminal as an inexplicable blemish on an otherwise immaculate record of human endeavor. He seemed to regard the capture and conviction of these saboteurs as his main purpose in life.

"We've got something," he told Amanda gravely. "A car dumped in Whiteman's Valley. It appeared to have suspicious stains and Uniform couldn't trace the owner so we brought it in. Hit the jackpot."

He handed over a forensic report that made Amanda smile. She'd given orders for samples to be taken from every abandoned car in the North Island, their owners to be traced and identities fed into the inquiry database.

"It's a match," Shaw declared. "Hair and blood type."

She scanned the report. Strands of hair had been

lifted from the front seat upholstery, traces of blood were found on the dashboard and the floor. The grouping of the stains was consistent with blood dripping from a serious head wound whilst the injured party was slumped across the dash.

Amanda recalled the massive depression behind "Mary's" left ear. "Who owns the car?"

"Bruce James Donnelly, twenty-four, artist. According to his mother, he's in Sydney. Bondi Beach. Left New Zealand the week before Christmas."

"And we haven't had a dumping since then," Amanda mused out loud. "Notify Sydney. We've got enough to bring him in for questioning."

"There's something else." Shaw passed her a photocopied sheet. "This arrived in your fan mail."

Amanda scanned the letter impassively. "What do you think?"

"We should look at this one. There are several features which differentiate it from the usual crank letters. First off, he's used a word processor. Then there are his references to you. These are not the usual lewd and salacious rubbish."

Amanda perused the relevant sentences. One jumped out at her.

Cocky bitch, aren't you? There won't be any medals where you're headed.

The tone was defensive, the threat implicit.

"Note the writer refers to the third victim as 'she,'" Shaw pointed out.

Amanda lifted her eyes. "McDougall's theory." The pathologist had concluded that despite the appearance of "Mary's" remains before those of

"Boris," she was not the second victim but the third. "Boris" had been frozen, but "Mary" hadn't.

"Has the press picked up on this?" Amanda asked.

Shaw shook his head. "I checked all the dailies. They don't seem to have noticed. The only people who know about 'Mary' are us and the killer."

"If Donnelly's our man this doesn't tie in," Amanda said, noting the Wellington postmark.

"All the same . . ." Austin frowned.

"Sure." Amanda nodded. It was way too early to make assumptions, but the car was their first big break. It would be almost too simple if its owner turned out to be the killer.

She pocketed the photocopy. "Send it away for psycholinguistic analysis."

They probably wouldn't glean much from only one communication, but maybe he'd write again. The message-sending type usually did.

"This appears to be the first communication," Shaw commented. "So if it's genuine you think our man is feeling some heat?"

Some experts viewed letters as distress signals, an expression of a killer's subconscious desire to be caught. Or they could be a response, triggered by events. Amanda considered the possibility. Something had prompted the killer to write. Her medal? The mere fact that he had mentioned it suggested resentment. It made sense in the context of serial killer profiles. These twisted individuals often craved public recognition, thriving on the media attention their crimes attracted and the anti-hero status implied by such sobriquets as "The Garbage Dump Killer."

So, Amanda thought, *maybe you're pissed that I got the front page last week and you didn't.*

She met Shaw's intent blue eyes and said reflectively, "If this is from him, I'm betting he'll dump again soon. He'd hate us to forget about him."

Ricky Hippolyte was picked up carrying five thousand dollars and a few snorts of coke. Joe had him stashed in an interview room.

"You're in a lot of trouble," Amanda told him softly.

Ricky stuck out his chin. "I won't say nothing till my lawyer's here."

Amanda shrugged. "I understand your lawyer's in Auckland and he's due back tomorrow. That's okay. We can put you up overnight."

"Now hold on a minute." He thumped the table, but not forcefully enough to hurt his fist. "You can't keep me in here. Not without a charge or nothin'."

"We're preparing a list of charges right at this moment. Of course it will take a while. The typist's at dinner. Meantime, like the Sergeant said, you're charged with possession."

"Get my lawyer on the phone right now," he demanded.

"You've already talked to the guy, Hippolyte," the Sergeant reminded him in a flat nasal tone. "Shall we take him downstairs then, ma'am?"

Amanda nodded. "Don't put him in with that Central Park weirdo though. I want to see him in one piece tomorrow."

"Who?" Ricky's cool dissolved into a frantic stare.

The Sergeant ignored him. "Got no choice, ma'am. We're real crowded. Constable Fenton will keep an eye on him. Look in every half hour or so."

"I don't want him messed up," Amanda warned. "We don't need the negative publicity."

Ricky was hammering the table to get their attention. "Wotcha talkin' about? Who's this Central Park dude anyway?"

"Keep quiet!" the Sergeant barked at him and called in a couple of his boys. "Take him below."

"No!" Ricky yelled. "I want to see my lawyer."

"He'll be here tomorrow," Amanda said sweetly. "Good luck down there."

She watched on a TV remote as they led Ricky through the familiar yellow painted steel and concrete walls of the underground holding cells. Voices echoed from behind the steel doors on either side. Right at the end of the passage was a room painted pink. It was the one they used for violent offenders. Pink was supposed to calm them down.

Ricky obviously had his own theory about the color coding. "No," he yelped as they opened the door. "Not in there. Not the queers' room."

He landed on the floor, sniveling. Straight above him dangled a sole lightbulb. It was painted pink like everything else in the cell.

Sitting on one of the two mattresses was a fat type with mean eyes and a crewcut. He looked up at Ricky and grinned wetly. "What profane wretch art thou?"

"She-it," Ricky bolted for the door, yelling into the grid. "Tell Miss Valentine I'll talk. Get me outta here now an' I'll tell her everything."

Howls emitted from the other cells. A voice whispered in Ricky's ear. "Poor fool and knave, I have one part in my heart that's sorry yet for thee."

Ricky pushed the bulky figure across the room. "Get your hands off me, scum. I got a friend who'll break every bone in your body."

"Lo, where he comes," crooned the slug.

Ricky banged on the door again. "Fuckin' pervert," he muttered.

"Why, what a monstrous fellow thou art, thus to rail on one that is neither known of thee nor knows thee!" The slug hoicked into a corner. "O, there has been much throwing about of brains." He hoicked again, staring at Ricky with those muddy little eyes. "Murder most foul," he announced.

"Help!" Ricky screamed out the grille. "Officer. Come quick."

The slug paced the cell restlessly. "Oh wretched state! Oh bosom black as death!"

"Stay back or I'll break your neck, fatso," said Ricky, trying to sound mean.

The slug advanced. "Now I could drink hot blood," he promised with a grunt. "And do such bitter business as the day would quake to look on."

Ricky bashed at the door until his fists were bruised and bleeding.

A voice outside ordered, "Quiet down in there."

"Help!" Ricky screamed as the slug breathed down on him. "Rape!"

"That's what they all say," someone laughed in another cell.

The door opened.

"But soft! What light through yonder window breaks?" the slug exclaimed.

Amanda stood there, legs spread, hands on hips. "They said you were asking for me, Ricky."

CHAPTER NINE

On her way home Amanda committed grievous bodily harm. She pulled into McDonald's and ordered a big everything. She had the decency to leave it untouched on the passenger seat till she got indoors. There she transferred her food onto a plate and dignified the fries with a sprinkle of origanum.

There was still some coffee left from the morning. Amanda shoved a cupful into the microwave and listened to her calls.

Roseanne. *Hi there, stranger. Are you in deep*

cover or something? Phone me or I'll file a missing persons report.

Her mother against a backdrop of Hawaiian music. *Honey, are you still alive down there? I rang your goddamned father I was so worried. You know who I ran into — Matt Robinson and he told me to tell you to get your ass back here. He's been elected DA and he says you just name the day. Come back home, honey. It's been long enough.* Thanks, Mom. I hear what you're saying. Kelly's been dead five years. Long enough.

The deli. Different voice. Female, husky, a little tentative. A new girl. *Hello. It's Linda from the delicatessen. Your order will be delivered at eight PM Friday and comes to ninety-four eighty. Oh, and Mr. Goldblum says did they like the sushi down at the station?* There was laughter in the voice. Maybe she would go pick up the order herself, Amanda thought.

Another female voice. *Amanda, hi. Debby Daley. I need to see you about the show. I'll drop by tonight after work.*

Shit. Amanda looked at her watch. Nine o'clock. With any luck Debby would have come earlier and missed her.

She gathered up her Big Mac and coffee, slunk into the sitting room and turned on the television. She was just in time for a Hill Street Blues rerun. Uninspired, she switched it off again and bit into her burger. It was room temperature and the lettuce was limp. The doorbell rang before she could start on her fries.

Debby Daley stood there wearing jeans and no

makeup. "Hi." She smiled cautiously. "Can I come in?"

"Sure." Amanda tried not to gape. "I'm sorry," she apologized in a dry tone, "I hardly recognized you without the cleavage."

Wincing, Debby walked ahead of her into the sitting room. Her backside looked even better in jeans than the little pink dress. "Hot, isn't it?" she commented.

Amanda gave a guilty start. "The weather . . . yes." She remembered her manners. "Uh, um, can I get you something to drink?"

"No." Debby's eyes took in the half-eaten meal. "I'm sorry. I'm interrupting you. Shall I come back later?" She seemed awkward, much younger.

"No, stay. If you can cope with watching me eat junk food, that is."

"Go right ahead. I don't want to disturb you." Debby drew her knees together and folded her hands neatly in her lap, glancing about the room with an expression of timid interest. "I was worried about coming here," she burst out suddenly. "I mean I thought you might be angry."

"Why should I be angry?" Amanda said mildly. "I get home from a hard day's slog, finally get to eat something and the next minute guests arrive. Here." She offered Debby her plate. "Have a fry."

Debby waved it away. "You are angry. I'll go. I'll phone you in the morning."

"Suit yourself," Amanda said.

With a brief reproachful glance, Debby gathered up the thin coat she'd hung over the chair.

Feeling a little ashamed of her rudeness, Amanda stalled her. "Why did you come here, anyway? Have you got something on this drug story?"

"It'll keep." Debby's voice was husky, her eyes downcast.

The woman was crying, drat her. Amanda heaved an impatient sigh. "For goodness sake, sit down. I'll get you a coffee."

Debby hovered uncertainly in the middle of the room, hands clasped to her chest. Either she was a woman of many parts or a damned good actress, Amanda decided. Whatever the case, she wasn't up to coping with a weeping routine.

"Here." She had located a box of Kleenex and corralled Debby back into her chair. "Blow your nose."

Grabbing a handful of fries, she loped off into the kitchen to brew some fresh coffee. "What's the problem?" she asked as she fumbled with the machine.

"Oh, I've just had a bad day." Forlorn laugh. "You know the sort. When you feel like you must be jinxed or something and everyone around you acts like a moron."

"I know exactly what you mean." Amanda returned with their coffees.

"People always think TV is so glamorous and I'm so lucky to have my own show," Debby went on. "But honestly, sometimes I feel like throwing it all in."

"It's a free world. I'm sure there are plenty of women out there who'd be happy to step out of lousy paid jobs and into your shoes."

"You think I'm ungrateful," Debby mumbled.

"I didn't say that."

"You meant it though."

Amanda stifled a long-suffering groan. This was starting to feel like a set-up. She changed the subject. "You look quite different without your makeup."

Debby raised self-conscious hands to her face. "Different? You mean plain?"

Amanda licked salt and origanum off her fingertips and studied the woman opposite her. The face was a perfect oval interrupted only by a slightly wayward chin, a little too stubborn for the first impression of pliant beauty. The eyes too were a surprise, wide and bright, deep aquamarine. Way too intelligent for the girly voice and fake smiles. Way too interesting, Amanda decided brutally. Self-preservation guided her next remark. "Plain? I guess you could say that."

Debby's shoulders drooped. "You don't think I'm attractive?"

"What does it matter? I'm sure men find you very attractive."

Debby laughed. It was over-pitched. "Men! I don't care what men think. I want to know what you think."

Amanda's pulse clamored in her ears. This was exactly the kind of conversation she couldn't afford to have with the Debby Daleys of this world. She might just as well go on air and announce she was a dyke. "I'll be honest with you, Debby," she said coolly. "I don't go for blondes."

"Blondes," Debby's voice wavered. "And that's it?"

Amanda nodded.

"But you do go for women, don't you?" Debby said unevenly.

Amanda gave her a measuring look. "You of all people should know why I can't answer that."

"You don't trust me."

"You're a reporter, Debby. And I'm a cop."

"Does that have to make us natural enemies? I'm also a woman. And I find you very attractive. I'd like to go to bed with you."

Amanda got to her feet. "I'll pretend you never said that. Now shall I walk you to the door?"

"No! Please," Debby intercepted her. "Can't we just pretend for ten minutes that we're not who we are? Can't we talk like ordinary women for once?"

"Why?" Amanda demanded sharply. "So you can get the personal angle?"

"No! This is not about angles for chrissakes. I like you, I want to get to know you. Do I have to quit my job or something to make you believe that? You've been a cop too long!"

"What the hell would you know about that!" Amanda retorted.

"It's obvious. You're so fucking paranoid." Debby wiped an arm across her eyes. Her lashes were spiked with tears. "I'm not here to trap you. I don't have to sink that low for a story."

"It's easy to say that now," Amanda's voice was rising. "But what about when it's over? Do you think I'll want to read all about my sexual performance in the Christmas issue of the Women's Weekly?"

"What makes you so damned sure it would be worth writing about?" Debby shouted.

"Well, you'll never know! I'm not about to risk my career for the sake of a fling with some blonde lust object. I'm not that desperate."

"Aren't you!" Debby stamped her foot. "Aren't you really?" Hands on hips, she glared at Amanda. "I think you're completely desperate. You don't trust anyone, do you? Not even yourself. That must be terrible. I feel sorry for you."

Blood pounded inside Amanda's head. "Save it," she said. Her voice sounded strange. "I'm happy."

"Compared to what!" Debby laughed mirthlessly. "A rock maybe? I suppose the next thing you'll tell me is that your job keeps you completely satisfied."

Amanda paused, engrossed suddenly in the hectic color flooding Debby's cheeks, the exquisite curve of her mouth. "No, not completely," she said with a trace of irony.

Debby fell silent, staring at her. Then she reached up and twisted at her hair. A blonde wig came away in her hands. "So you don't fancy blondes," she said softly. "How about this, then?"

Amanda swallowed a gasp. Debby Daley had short straight black hair. If anything, she looked even more stunning than before. Amanda couldn't think of anything she'd rather do than drag her into the sack. But she would have to be an intellectual pygmy to consider it. Even if Debby were the genuine article, a lesbian who wore drag on her talk show, where would it all lead? A couple of months of great sex, then goodbye and an embittered Debby shares her sorrow with the nation ... I was seduced by a queer cop (flutter, sob).

Debby had closed the distance between them, the

wig sliding to the floor. "Make love with me, Amanda," she whispered, linking her hands behind Amanda's neck.

Amanda gently disengaged herself. "I'm sorry, Debby." It was the truth, she realized with sharp regret.

"You're not sorry at all." Debby said stonily. "You couldn't give a damn. You think you're the one who's got everything to lose. Do you have any idea what would happen to me if this got out? Curtains!" She moved across the room and gathered up her belongings. "I took a risk coming here," she said shakily. "But I thought you might be worth it. Looks like I was wrong!" Barging past Amanda, she headed for the front door.

"You left your hair on the floor," Amanda said quietly.

Debby halted, swung around. "Keep it!" she hissed. "By the time I've run your show you'll need a disguise to go to the supermarket!"

Amanda's jaw dropped. "The show?"

Debby shrugged. "Oh, I nearly forgot. That was what I came here to tell you before I decided to make a fool of myself. Your interview is on the air at seven tomorrow."

"Tomorrow! But you said you'd hold off."

"You didn't believe me, did you? I mean really, Amanda. This is the media." She wrenched the door open and smiled acid sweet. "Enjoy it, won't you?"

Dazed, Amanda watched her slam the door of her white BMW convertible and depart in a trail of scalded rubber.

* * * * *

When Amanda got into the Accounts Department
the next morning, the heat was on. They were
working on it, Margaret explained. Getting it sorted
out before winter set in. The younger woman had
stripped right down to a singlet and skirt and she
was fanning herself with a set of balance sheets.

Amanda sank into her swivel chair and gazed
listlessly at the Degas print above Lillian Bennett's
door. She'd had a lousy sleep and it didn't improve
her temper any to look down and see the evidence of
her folly stuffed into a plastic bag under her desk.
She nudged it further away, ignoring the blonde
hairs that spilled out onto the floor, and grimly
dialed the TV studios for the third time.

"I'm afraid Miss Daley is not taking calls at the
moment," the secretary said.

"Did you leave my name?"

"I certainly did, ma'am."

"Please try again. It's police business."

"I'm sorry, Inspector Valentine, but Miss Daley is
in a meeting and cannot be disturbed unless it's
urgent."

Frustration seeped into her tone. "It is urgent! I
need to contact Miss Daley now."

"Would you care to make an appointment?"

"No!" Amanda said tersely.

"Then I cannot assist you any further," the
secretary said. Amanda was certain she detected a
note of satisfaction in the polished tone.

Swearing loudly, she dropped the phone back into
its cradle. A young records clerk pushing a file

trolley into the room covered a nervous titter and started to back out again.

"It's all right," Amanda said irritably. "Come on in."

She should be used to the way the junior staff cowered around her, she supposed; used to conversation drying up when she entered a room. Her attempts at friendliness had only seemed to engender even more suspicion. She was a homicide detective assigned to the Mayor's Office. Everyone around her seemed to be waiting for a body to be discovered, possibly their own.

"Will there be anything else, Inspector Valentine?" the junior stammered, shifting her center of balance from one foot to the other.

"Sit down." Amanda indicated a chair and the girl hurried to comply, gazing wide-eyed at Amanda.

"I'm going to ask you to do something very important," Amanda said briskly. "Tell me, do you drive?"

"I've got a Mini."

Amanda stared at the girl's legs, then shook herself. She was talking about her car for godsake. She grabbed her notepad and scrawled a greasy apology to Debby Daley. Maybe it still wasn't too late to stop the show going to air. "Do you know where the Avalon TV Studios are?" she asked.

Lunch hour was a loose affair at the City Council. In the Mayor's chambers no one would be missed for at least two hours. It was the perfect time for a killing. Maybe someone would pop Lillian, Amanda reflected. At least she wouldn't be short of suspects. It was like that with unpopular victims. A veritable banquet of leads.

She entertained herself with that sick train of thought as she strolled along the hot pavement to the trendy coffee joint down the road. The place had hard chairs and crawled with out of work actors and downwardly mobile community lawyers. Loud rap music played non-stop, forcing diners to shout above it between mouthfuls of their vegetarian cuisine.

Joe was waiting twitchily at the self-serve counter. "Christ," he greeted her. "I could go a decent steak."

"The pizza's good here."

Joe examined it dubiously. "No pepperoni."

"I'm having a tofuburger."

"That got steak in it?"

"No."

Joe piled his plate up with baked potatoes. "Shrimp," he explained, pointing at the topping. "Seems it's okay to kill them."

The man at the counter served their coffees with an air of exquisite martyrdom and carried them ahead of Amanda to a vacant table. Both cups overflowed as he put them down.

"How are things shaping up at the Mayor's Office?" Joe demanded. "You gonna be outta there soon?"

"I sure hope so. I'm getting lazy and careless just so I can feel at home."

"Bob Welch's been acting like a dog with two dicks since you went over. He's on the Kero Dero case now. Reckons he'll clear it by Friday."

Amanda rolled her eyes. "Must be hell for him with all those eye-witnesses."

"Purgatory," Joe said. "I hear Hippolyte spilled his guts."

"One look at Marty and he couldn't talk fast enough. All that stuff about blood and brains."

Joe laughed. "The old Son of Hamlet routine. Yeah, I saw that at the Charity Ball last year. The kid's a genius, ain't he? Learns it all in the amateur operatics."

"He's wasted in Uniform Branch," Amanda observed. "I've recommended him for CIB training."

"So, learn anything about Jezebel?"

"Hippolyte swears he didn't do it. I think he's telling the truth."

"So how come she fingered him?"

"This is where it gets interesting. Take a look." She flipped out a photograph of the suit Ricky met in the Library. "Christopher Alan Clarke, aged thirty-four, car salesman, divorced, no kids, clean record."

"Your average yuppie."

"Right," Amanda said. "Except he's Hippolyte's boss."

"You mean Hippolyte's selling cars?"

"No, the little creep's selling girls and playing errand boy." She handed Joe a customs and immigration record for Christopher Clarke.

"The guy's taken a shine to Bangkok," he remarked. "Six trips in twelve months."

"Maybe no one grovels for him here," Amanda said dryly.

"You mean sex tours?" Joe looked dumbstruck.

"That's probably a perk. But according to Hippolyte he's there to buy women for a couple of places he runs over here."

"How the hell does he get them through immigration?"

"I was wondering that too. Brings them in as domestic labor, I guess."

Joe scratched his head. "So where does Jezebel fit in?"

"Hippolyte claims Clarke asked him to find someone who could run one of the brothels. He thought of Jezebel and took her out to a place in Eastbourne to meet Clarke. Evidently Jezebel didn't like the look of the setup and said no. Later, she tries some blackmail scam. Threatens to sell her story to the press."

"So Clarke decides to shut her up? The beating was a warning?"

"That's what Hippolyte thinks. It's Clarke's style, evidently."

"Charming. So, what's next? We talk to this Clarke individual?"

"Yes, but kid glove treatment. Clarke could be the connection we're looking for. I have some interesting data on the guy from another source. He likes his recreational drugs."

"Rich customer?"

"My source thinks he supplies."

Joe chewed on that one.

Amanda could guess what he was thinking. "I'm not handing this over to Vice," she said.

"You think Jezebel's in over her head?"

"That's something I want to find out. Before we talk to Mr. Clarke."

CHAPTER TEN

Jezebel acted the airhead queen. "Chris Clarke? Not one of my johns."

"Never met him?"

"Don't think so."

"That's not what Ricky told me." Amanda dragged her chair closer. "Talk ..." she said softly.

Jezebel muttered some deprecating remark and twitched at the lace on her sleeves. "He took me in one of them fancy limousines," she said dejectedly. "Pure white. Made me feel like a bride."

"Took you where?"

"Eastbourne someplace."

"The brothel?"

Jezebel looked scandalized. "That scum wanted me to run the show for him. I told him where to stick it. Lovie, the place was full of foreign girls, you know, *Asians*."

"Illegal immigrants?"

"Illegal everything," Jezebel sniffed.

"So you told Clarke no?"

Jezebel nodded, avoiding Amanda's eyes.

"What's with the bully boy stuff then?"

"I don't know what you mean." She came across pathetic and hounded.

"Don't lie to me," Amanda said angrily. "Ricky told me you were blackmailing Clarke."

"That little turd."

"What have you got on him, Jezebel?"

"Nothing! I got nothing on him. I told that boy I was gonna sell my story to the papers, that's all."

"Don't play games with me!" Amanda hissed. "They were there looking for something at your place, weren't they?"

Jezebel shook her head, refusing to be drawn out.

Frustrated, Amanda said urgently. "I'm trying to protect you, Jezebel. I know you're in trouble. Please, tell me about Clarke."

Jezebel shrank back into her pillows. All of a sudden, she seemed very old and brittle. "Lovie, I told you already," she said vaguely. "Truth is I hope you get the scum. That's what they're paying you for."

* * * * *

Twenty-eight Sorrento Drive was a ritzy address on the moneybelt of Wellington. The street curved gracefully along the top of Oriental Bay, affording its residents panoramic views of the harbor and city. It looked like a luxury car lot: wall to wall Mercs, the occasional BMW — the wife's shopping basket; — or Porsche — a man needs his toys. Every home had a manicured lawn and a guard dog sporting a studded collar and baring its teeth at passers-by.

"What's our approach?" Joe asked as they parked outside Chris Clarke's mansion.

"We don't have anything connecting him directly to the beating," Amanda replied, "so it's routine inquiries."

Joe whistled at the impressive Mediterranean-style structure beyond the electronic gates. "Makes a buck."

"For a pimp, you mean?" Amanda stated their business into the intercom and the gates parted to admit them.

He doesn't deserve it, she decided, as they approached the main entrance. This was the kind of view that lodged itself in the subconscious, anchoring one to a time or place the way some songs do. Across the shimmering harbor, the city basked shadowless in the late January sun. Cars proceeded with antlike purpose along the myriad arteries that fed into the heart of the capital, and overhead, gulls rose high and motionless on the thermals of another windless day.

"Postcard, ain't it?" Joe commented, wiping a fine mist of lawn spray off his face.

"It better be," a voice came from behind them.

"Round here it's a million for the view and two-fifty grand for the house."

Instant dislike, Amanda reflected. It was a curious phenomenon. Scientists attributed it to pheromones, those minute chemical secretions that attract or repel. Whatever the explanation, Amanda could understand straightaway why Debby had categorized Chris Clarke as a creep.

Clarke was shirtless and wearing faded Levis. His reptilian eyes flicked across Amanda with the assurance of a man who expects women to find him sexy.

"I'm Chris Clarke," he said, sliding a thumb into his pocket. "You officers use a drink?"

Amanda surveyed him coolly. "No thank you, Mr. Clarke. This isn't a social call. I'm Detective Inspector Amanda Valentine and this is my colleague, Detective Sergeant Joe Moller."

"I believe you." Clarke smirked without glancing at their IDs.

"We're carrying out routine inquiries in connection with an assault," Amanda said formally. "May we speak inside?"

Clarke wasn't buying. "Personally, I prefer fresh air," he drawled. "Come and take a pew."

Extending along the rear of the house was the classic swimming pool and decking, complete with Italian outdoor furniture. Clarke bypassed a shade umbrella, and indicated a table and chairs. "Sure you won't have that drink?"

Watching stranded insects treading water on the

glassy pool surface, Amanda shook her head. "I believe you are acquainted with a Miss Jezebel Matenga," she said, taking the chair opposite Clarke.

Catching her eye, Joe wandered off, hands in pockets, saying, "Nice place you got here, Mr. Clarke. Mind if I take a stroll?"

Clarke shot him a single, calculating glance, then returned his attention to Amanda, seemingly satisfied that Joe was just another nosey cop.

"Miss Matenga?" Amanda prompted.

"Can't say the name means anything."

Amanda stared at him. "How long have you lived here, Mr. Clarke?"

"Too long." He snapped the tab on a Fosters. "Been thinking about a move . . ."

"Really?"

"Sydney maybe . . . slice of the action."

"What line of work are you in?"

He paused. "The hospitality industry."

"Miss Matenga mentioned you offered her a job."

"I turn over a few staff."

No doubt. Amanda leaned a fraction toward him, her gaze unfaltering. "I know you run girls, Mr. Clarke. In fact, I know a great deal about your operations. I could close you down tomorrow, and maybe I will." She caught the giveaway dilation of his pupils and produced a dazzling smile. "Or maybe I won't. You want to talk about it, give me a call." Dropping her card on the table, she signaled Joe.

As Clarke's gates closed silkily behind them, Joe observed, "That was quick."

Amanda grinned. "That was what Moira McDougall would call a rise. Now we just have to wait and see if he bites."

An hour later Amanda was grinding her teeth at the Mayor's Office. It was slow progress pawing through the papers Lillian had thrust at her. Nonetheless it was obvious why Michael Wilson hadn't made it a priority to hire an internal auditor.

The guy was not exactly Mr. Clean. His expense account spending was worth double his salary and most of it wasn't supported by receipts. Then there were the contracts. Michael Wilson held key positions on most of the Council's major works committees. As Amanda grappled with minutes, planning documents, building plans and tenders, a clear pattern emerged.

Wilson regularly overturned committee decisions without apparent reason. Lillian had helpfully marked the most dramatic instances with pink highlighter.

Amanda asked her what was going on.

Clearly Lillian thought it was a dumb question. "He's letting contracts to the brethren, of course. Just look at the Wharf Development.

"You mean the Marble Palace?"

That was what everyone called it. The Wharf Development was the biggest project the Council had ever undertaken, the conversion of acres of disused wharf to an upscale retail and apartment complex. It was mega-dollar territory.

Originally the committee in charge of the project had commissioned designs around a kind of

Montmarte concept. Soft stone, winding cobbled pathways, tiny specialist boutiques. Six weeks ago, at the hands of the Deputy Mayor, the Parisian influence had given way to an ionic wonderland.

Marble, Amanda noted. Marble everything: towering columns, reproductions of the statue of David and the Venus de Milo, marble urinals in the men's rooms.

Lillian had an explanation. "Guess who owns a marble quarry."

"Wilson?"

"He's not that stupid." Lillian cast a grim eye over her shoulder pad. "It's all in his wife's name ... her maiden name of course — oldest trick in the book. Look up the company's register. Harriet Cluny, that's her."

"Does anyone else know about this?" Amanda said.

Lillian pursed her coral lips. "Only poor Harvey."

Amanda figured she meant Harvey Perkins, the Mayor. "So can't he just overrule Wilson?" she asked. "I mean, he is the Mayor."

Lillian fell silent, then she beckoned Amanda close. "That's the problem, dear. He can't do a thing. And it's all thanks to that little tramp Angelique Le Bon."

"Angelique?" Amanda wasn't sure if she wanted to hear any more. After all, she could always tune into *Days of Our Lives* if she really needed a drama fix.

But Lillian's thin chest was heaving with indignation. "She used to be a typist here, if you could call two fingers typing. Threw herself at the

Mayor's head, wouldn't leave him alone. Finally poor Harvey sacked her, but before she left she wrote some pack of lies about how Harvey ... How she and Harvey ..."

"I see," Amanda said. "So where are the allegations?"

"Where do you think?" Lillian said darkly. Sucking in her cheeks and smoothing her aqua linen skirt over her bony hips, she pronounced, "Poor Harvey. He's nurtured a viper at his bosom."

"Poor Harvey" was leaving Michael Wilson's office as Amanda approached. The Mayor was a short solid man with a springy gait and square, capable hands. Amongst the city's intelligentsia he was something of a joke, the former plumber who'd made a fortune out of other people's leaking toilets. My dear, the fellow thinks opera is some black woman on afternoon television. To the working population however, Harvey Perkins was seen as a man who knew what an honest day's work was about, who understood the issues that affected ordinary people.

He nodded pleasantly as Amanda passed him, but his knuckles were white over clenched fists and there was a strained look about his eyes. The Mayor was obviously deeply disturbed over something.

Amanda thought about Angelique Le Bon and decided rashly that Harvey Perkins was not the kind of man who would rat on his wife or molest his staff. She wondered how much Michael Wilson had paid the girl to provide him with a lever that could destroy Perkin's election credibility.

114

Wilson's door was ajar and Amanda lifted her hand to knock, then lowered it as she heard a voice raised angrily. A one-sided conversation was in progress. Wilson was evidently on the phone.

"— Well, it's not my fucking problem," Amanda heard. "Ring me at home for God's sake. I can't talk here."

A pause. "She what! I don't like this. It's gone too bloody far already."

More silence. "I know, I know. I want out too, buddy ... Okay. I'll talk to him. Just stay cool. We're nearly there."

The phone was slammed down amidst a string of curses. Amanda gave it a moment, then knocked.

"Inspector Valentine." Wilson flashed an adman's smile that successfully erased any evidence of his true feelings. "This is a great pleasure." He got to his feet, hand extended, in a solicitous display of good manners.

It was impossible to avoid comparing him with the man she'd just passed. Where the Mayor was grey and crumpled, Michael Wilson was smooth-cheeked, fragrant, and expensively clad; an image consultant's success story.

Amanda made a point of mauling his hand a little, and for a split second his photogenic features registered a kind of startled embarrassment. Then he was back to his cosmopolitan self.

"What can I do for you, Inspector?"

Taking the chair he had indicated — one facing his desk — Amanda said glibly, "I'm looking into HRM document retrieval at the moment. And I'm asking all senior managers to return any personnel files they're holding."

Wilson's hand flicked to his school tie and he made a show of leafing through the papers on his desk. "I don't believe I have any ..."

"According to the records section you have one." Amanda took a slip of paper from her pocket and read, "Angelique Le Bon."

This stopped him dead. "Angelique?" A trace of color seeped into his cheeks. "I don't think so ..."

"In your drawers or your filing cabinet?" Amanda offered helpfully.

Wilson turned narrowed blue eyes on her. "I said it's not here."

Catching her expression, he recovered himself with a plastic smile. "But I'll ask the girls to have a look for it this afternoon."

"Perhaps I can save them the trouble." Amanda got to her feet, one hand brushing lightly across a pile of papers on his desk.

A muscle jerked in the corner of one of his eyes. His hands were trembling slightly, Amanda noted. Washington twitch — back home a characteristic of the denizens of Capitol Hill. Beneath his carefully constructed campaign front, Michael Wilson was definitely jumpy.

She turned up the heat a little. "I'll start with the filing cabinet."

"No!" He lurched to his feet.

Amanda lifted her eyebrows.

"It is here after all," he covered unevenly. "I'll get it for you." He foraged in his bottom drawer, eventually extracting a thin file which he passed to Amanda.

Thanking him crisply, she glanced around the spacious office. It was twice the size of the Mayor's and lavishly decorated. As she left, the phone rang again and she guessed from Wilson's honeyed tone that it was his wife.

You poor woman, she found herself thinking.

As soon as she got back to her desk she opened the file. There wasn't much there. Angelique Le Bon had only worked at the Council for two months. The topmost sheet was a copy of her final pay slip. But above it, caught on the file pin, was a shred of white paper.

Someone had pulled a sheet out of Angelique's file in a big hurry. Paydirt, Amanda decided happily, then she cupped her forehead dejectedly in her hand. What the hell was she doing on some political bootlicking mission at the Mayor's Office when real crime was happening out there? The Garbage Dump Killer had probably started on his next victim by now. Bob Welch probably had his feet on her desk . . .

She phoned Austin Shaw. "Any news on Donnelly?"

"They haven't got him yet. But there's something else. McDougall found some shell fragments on the car floor."

"Bullets?" None of the victims had been shot.

"No. Seashells. Little pieces. And sand. No great quantity — caught in the tread of a shoe, I'd say."

"What's Donnelly's address?"

"Palmerston North."

"No beaches there. Where do the samples originate?"

"The DSIR say it's one of the Gold Coast beaches, Waikenae or Paekakariki."

Amanda considered a possible scenario involving the unknown Donnelly. He had been trolling for victims away from his home locale. This predatory pattern was a hallmark of the serial killer. He picked up "Mary." Killed her somewhere near the beach — Queen Elizabeth Park maybe. Took a walk on the beach to wash his hands and get rid of some evidence. Then he returned to Palmerston North, dismembered and bagged the body and stashed it in his fridge. A couple of days later, he drove to Wellington, left "Mary" and the garbage dump, got rid of the car and flew across the Tasman with the Christmas exodus.

"Get a warrant and search Donnelly's last address," Amanda ordered. "And send a couple of men up the coast door-to-door. Circulate that sketch of 'Mary' and ask about the car."

In a tiny, conservative, seaside township, people remembered strangers. They noticed unusual events. They would be hard pressed to forget a woman with a tattoo on her shoulder or a rusted Holden station wagon with a bumper sticker that read JESUS SAVES ... STAMPS.

CHAPTER ELEVEN

Amanda inched her way across to the edge of the bed and suspended a leg over the side. Her skin prickled as its film of sweat began to evaporate. 1:00 AM. Had she slept at all?

Peeling the sheets off her body, she swung her other leg out and sat up. Every crease felt sticky. Her armpits reeked, her thighs clung damply together and a trickle of moisture was oozing its way from beneath her breasts.

Sluggishly she paced to her window and opened it wide. The night was vast and hot. Sodium streetlights cast pallid pools along the empty sidewalks, and somewhere blocks away a cat fight was in progress.

Amanda felt edgy. Her heart suddenly jumped a beat. What was the matter with her? Was it just the heat? Or was it something more serious? Advanced caffeine addiction, early menopause, sexual frustration? A feeling of presentiment clawed sharply at her insides and she glanced at the phone, almost expecting it to ring. She could call Joe, she thought. But what for? Irritated, she opened a drawer, extracted some clothing and crept from her room.

She turned the shower on cool and tilted her face to the jets, all but swooning with relief. Closing her eyes, she permitted her mind to roam.

What if Donnelly was a dead end? What if his car had been stolen and he didn't know a thing? She thought about the letter and felt an odd pulse of excitement — a sense that it was from him. *How did you like the show tonight?*

It was surprising what the subconscious regurgitated given the chance, she thought. Frequently it was the small things, the detail that leaked past the five senses to lodge in a thousand disordered fragments in the subterranean mind.

A good detective could exercise some control over this process. A great detective, Amanda thought heretically, could harness it. Detectives were trained to observe, to collect information — much of it random — and to think literally. Computers could take the legwork out of sorting and tagging data. But it still took more than analytical skills to solve certain crimes. Some detectives called it "getting lucky." Amanda called it "a hunch."

Toweling herself dry, she returned to pragmatism and the subject of Michael Wilson. The guy obviously had Harvey Perkins by the short and curlies. Was it really just over allegations of sexual misconduct by some typist? From the sounds of his phone call that afternoon, Wilson was wound up about something and wanted out.

She could certainly relate to that. She wanted out of the Council. Let the Chief find someone else to lubricate his relations with City Hall. Perhaps if she presented Mayor Perkins with a ticket to squeaky clean pre-election publicity, he'd be satisfied and she could get back to her life.

For starters, she needed to find Angelique Le Bon's statement, and Wilson was not about to hand it over. Amanda frowned at her next thought. *So help yourself to it.* No. It was insane to contemplate the idea. She couldn't just sneak into the Deputy Mayor's office and search the place. No crime had been committed, no warrant was in force.

She pulled on a lightweight black tracksuit and running shoes, loaded the Smith & Wesson, slid it home into her shoulder holster and glanced guiltily at her reflection in the mirror. *Don't even think about it,* she warned herself.

Windows down and stereo blasting voluptuous Chopin, she drove into the city. The streets were wet and shiny in the aftermath of the night truck. Amanda could imagine it chugging and swishing ahead of her, the driver leaning out his open cab, humming discordantly, the men in dungarees walking behind spearing McDonald's wrappers with spiked poles.

Amanda shot a red light so as to keep the breeze

coming. I'm the law, she told her conscience. She halted outside the Council Chambers, motor running. It was 1:30. Every window was lit up. Recognizing the shadowy figures passing between offices, she released a frustrated sigh. Her nocturnal raid had coincided with the cleaners.

For a moment she toyed with the idea of going up anyway, brazening out her presence as something to do with the security review. But what if someone mentioned it? How would she account for a search of Michael Wilson's office? Checking for electronic surveillance devices planted by dissident green Councilors?

Despondently, she pulled out and followed the one-way system onto Victoria Street. There she slowed, eyes narrowing as she was confronted with the arrows to Brooklyn. Suddenly her heart started to race. *Are you out there?* she whispered beneath her breath.

Guided by some inner logic, she crossed impulsively into the left lane and took the ten-minute drive to Happy Valley.

The Valley was a damp, misty cleft dividing the hills beyond Brooklyn. The area was optimistically described as the Greenbelt, but in reality it was motley unkempt land, gorse covered and wind blown. Amanda took a right below Hawkin's Hill, dimmed her lights, rolled up her windows and headed along potholed Landfill Road toward the checkpoint. At two in the morning it was unmanned, the barrier arm raised for the dawn arrival of the first council dump trucks.

She drove up the gravel, killing her lights as she neared the crest overlooking the dump. The night was pitch dark, and even with her windows up the odor was rank and fetid. Slowly her eyes grew accustomed to the darkness, focusing on several large shapes discernible below, earth-moving vehicles sitting idle until daybreak.

Amanda inched her window down a little and listened to the night. Paper rustled, gulls screeched the occasional protest, warning intruders off their patch. Amanda was certain she could hear the restless stirring of maggots and vermin among the tons of plastic and rotting food that formed the sordid hillside below. She listened harder, sifting out the ordinary hum of the dump ecology and tuning in to what remained: the odd metallic click of her car engine cooling, the soft pulse of the ocean in the distance, the distant whine of the occasional car passing through Happy Valley.

There it was. A peculiar, shuffling sound coming from somewhere below and to her right. Amanda located her torch and slowly, noiselessly, opened her door.

Stench greeted her in a hot, sickening wave. Gagging instinctively, she stepped out of her car and ran, crouching low, ten paces along the dusty road. The sound stopped and she froze, ears straining.

Hardly daring to breathe, she pulled her gun. There it was again. A definite shuffling, like something being dragged. It was accompanied by some kind of rasping breathing. The sounds were coming from directly below her. Amanda broke out in a cold sweat.

He'd killed three so far, their strangled, decapitated, and dismembered bodies discovered piece by gruesome piece buried under mounds of garbage.

Fear converted Amanda's insides to a writhing snake pit. Fighting it, she moved deliberately toward the edge of the road and zeroed in on the direction of the sounds. Nine feet and closing. She prepared herself psychologically for the worst. Don't panic. Shoot to disable.

Balancing her weight carefully, she knelt, pointed the torch in her left hand, and with her right, braced the gun across one knee, aimed, and hit the light.

There was a movement. The beam bounced off a pair of wild, liquid eyes, then a menacing form plunged straight out of the night at her. Even as she pumped bullets into it, Amanda recognized the face of a killer.

It fell at her feet, a full-grown pit bull terrier, as dangerous and unpredictable as any psychopath. For a long moment, she remained squatting beside the torn body, caught between pity — for this creature clad in the deceptive form of a dog — and a weak-kneed relief. What was the animal doing here? Scavenging, she supposed. It had probably been abandoned by owners who couldn't control it. The garbage dump was a popular destination for unwanted pets.

She got to her feet and shone the torch down the slope where the dog had been foraging. The beam played across a mess of indiscernible objects, plastic-shrouded lumps, twisted metal, fluttering ribbons of paper.

Slowly, she threaded her way down toward a couple of torn rubbish bags. The smell hit her first, then there was the clammy feeling crawling across her flesh, then her stomach lurched violently and saliva coursed across her tongue.

There, glistening darkly in the torchlight, was a semidevoured human head.

Amanda returned to her car and locked herself in, staring weakly at her radio. When her breathing permitted, she called Joe.

"You want me to guard this head for you till McDougall arrives?" he muttered sleepily.

"I'm going to cordon it off now, Joe. Can you get here soon?"

There was a lot of mumbling, then he said. "Where the hell are you off to?"

"I've got some business in town."

"You've lost me, kid. What are you doing prowling around the goddamned garbage dump at two in the morning anyway?"

"It was just a —"

"No!" he broke in. "Don't say it. I don't want to hear about hunches. A normal cop waits till the public reports a stiff, in daylight hours. A normal cop isn't creeping around the dump shooting up mad dogs and acting like a goddamn decoy." He sounded angry.

"Joe," Amanda said softly. "I didn't know you cared."

Fifteen minutes later she passed him coming the

other way on Landfill Road. They pulled up opposite each other and wound down their windows.

"Hot enough for you?" Joe asked. The smell of pizza wafted out of his car, turning Amanda's stomach.

"I've called Austin," she said. "He'll be down here with the forensic team at first light. Some Uniforms are on their way now."

"Where are you gonna be?"

"The Council."

Joe shook his head. "You're cracking up."

Maybe he was right, Amanda thought as she headed back into town.

It was 3:10 AM when she pulled in a block down from the Council Chambers. Dust rose around her as she bailed out of the car. Amanda knew she smelled disgusting. She seemed to have carried the dump away with her.

Inside the Council lobby, she headed straight for the elevators. A panel displayed keyholes and numbers for each floor and a red light above each indicated that it was locked. The light above the third floor was green, meaning someone was up there or had been recently.

Security inspected at 2:30 AM, she recalled. Maybe they were running late. Mentally rehearsing a likely story for the guard, she took the fire escape stairwell up.

Unlike Accounts, the third floor was carpeted. Important people had their offices there: the Town Clerk, the Chief Building Inspector, the Deputy

Mayor and the Councillors. Each had their name plaque on a heavy door.

Amanda paused in front of the last one and pulled on a pair of latex gloves. Reminding herself that she was the law, she tried the handle. It was open. Surprised, she knocked softly and went in.

Michael Wilson's desk drawers were conveniently unlocked, and Amanda rifled them for Angelique's statement. There was nothing. Undaunted, she moved to the filing cabinet and fingered her way along the suspended envelopes, seeking evidence of a hastily-filed sheet.

Passing a folder marked campaign, she extracted what looked like a proposal document from a PR firm and scanned the contents. It was riddled with phrases like image-building, man of integrity and pragmatic decision-making. A sentence leapt out at her: *Negative publicity attaching to the financial mismanagement of the present incumbent can only strengthen your position.*

Disgusted, she moved on through the drawers. What the hell was she doing here anyway, she wondered. Who did she think she was, nosing through the Deputy Mayor's private papers. Cops had been demoted for less.

Fending off the nauseating odor of garbage dump, she moved through the chaos of the bottom drawer, shoving her arm down between the suspended envelopes to grope beneath them. Her persistence was rewarded with a crumpled sheet of white paper. Catching the signature at the bottom, she stuffed it into her jacket and locked the filing cabinet.

It was only when she returned the cabinet key to its home in Wilson's desk that she noticed an odd burning smell. Mystified, she glanced around the office, seeking the source. Perhaps she was only smelling herself again, she thought wryly.

She looked at her watch. Three-thirty. She crossed to the door, turned and made a final sweep of the room, her eyes halting at the one thing out of the ordinary. Stooping, she plucked it from the carpet. A tiny white flower — gypsophylla — the kind brides carry.

She hadn't noticed flowers in Wilson's office that afternoon. Maybe he'd bought a bunch for his wife. Shrugging, she moved to the bin to get rid of it and stared down in astonishment. It was full of charred papers, a great sheaf of them.

The scorched remains were still slightly warm, and buried at the bottom of the heap were several legible sheets, saved apparently by the residue of water left when the cleaners last rinsed the bin.

Amanda retrieved the surviving pages and frowned in confusion. Michael Wilson had been in his office in the dead of night destroying a heap of legal documents. They had one thing in common. The name Christopher Clarke appeared on them.

CHAPTER TWELVE

The next morning, Amanda parked around the side entrance of the Station and sat for a moment in reflective inertia. Michael Wilson: respectable, clean-cut, family man and aspiring Mayor. According to the documents in his rubbish bin he'd had some kind of business relationship with Chris Clarke. What was their connection now?

Clarke ran brothels, had people beaten senseless and was possibly a Mr. Big in the drug trade. Hardly the kind of business associate a Mayoral candidate would want to advertise.

At the sound of voices, she glanced up. Two men had just walked out of the side door. She recognized the tall, stooping one immediately. Bob Welch. The men stopped. They appeared to be talking heatedly. Welch touched the shorter man's shoulder as he started to move away. Amanda's jaw went slack. The shorter man was Michael Wilson.

Casting a single backward glance, Wilson walked briskly down the alleyway to the main road. Amanda watched him disappear, then got out of her car and headed for the doorway. Bob Welch was still there and the eyes that met hers glittered with peculiar malice.

Not surprisingly, the station was abuzz with the events of the preceding night.

"We've penned up the autograph hunters downstairs," someone crowed as Amanda marched through. "What are we charging for the portrait photos?"

Amanda reminded herself to send a grenade to Debby Daley.

At the inquiry center most of the Big Mack Task Force were hanging over a video player. Amanda's heart sank as she heard herself. *They always slip up sometime because they can't resist showing off. You could say they are more egotistical than intelligent* . . .

Detective Janine Harrison, the most junior of Amanda's team, commented with awe, "They did this with the Son of Sam too — made him mad as hell."

"He was already mad, Harrison," Amanda said

blandly. "What they made him do was reveal himself."

Everyone turned to face her. Harrison blushed in the fetching way she did when Amanda spoke directly to her.

"Do you think he dumped the head last night because of the program?" someone asked.

"It's an interesting theory," Amanda said. "But we won't know when that head was dumped until we hear from the lab." She glanced at the faces around her. "Who's down at the dump?"

They sang out a few names, then one of the senior detectives commented, "We finished checking out those confessions. All crazies."

"That's just the beginning," Amanda muttered.

Sunday's mannequin fiasco had really set the crazies off. The media were wallowing in it, pigs in clover. And every nutcase in town was after a piece of the action. With any luck, some of them would get carried away and confess to crimes they had actually committed. Amanda reached McDougall's cellular phone. "What have we got?"

Moira McDougall laughed. "Well, for starters we've got one hundred degrees and climbing and one of the new boys is spewing his guts out ..."

"You got students on the job again?"

"Yes, so help me God. Hold on a minute ..."

Amanda heard her shouting instructions ... *Yes, you do have to bag the used sanitary towels the head's reposing on* ... "Good news. At a glance it looks like 'Boris' and this time we've got complete bridgework, gold fillings, no less. A week and we could have a name."

"Any unusual features?"

"No. Same deal exactly. The head was hacksawed off. Pinus radiata particles in the wound. Eyelids pinned."

"Any idea how long it's been there?"

"I've got good news and bad news."

"Gimme the bad news first," Amanda groaned.

"Okay. The bad news is that dog was eating a frozen dinner. I got here at three-thirty AM and the head wasn't fully thawed. My guess is you probably missed your killer by maybe an hour, tops —"

"Shit! Goddamn it!" Amanda caught Janine Harrison's startled eyes, and found herself wondering if she'd ever been that young.

"And the good news ..." Moira paused significantly. "He left his footprints."

"He what?"

"Your guy makes bigfoot look like a sylph. Size twelve, and that's a modest estimate."

"What makes you sure they're his?" Amanda exchanged a look with Austin Shaw.

The atmosphere in the room had undergone a tangible shift. Her team was gathered about in watchful silence, the young contingent even daring to look hopeful.

"Shell fragments," Moira said briskly. "Looks like the guy stood a few yards down from the road and tossed the head. Looks like he tracked through some paint thinnings on his way. Stood on a paper sack and ... behold."

"But that print could be anybody's, surely. The dump is full of broken shells," Amanda cautioned.

"Not this kind. Not alcithoe. That's a univalve species you'll only find on the Gold Coast beaches. It matches the sample taken from the car."

Amanda smiled. *Gotcha,* she thought.

Not a man to engage in premature backslapping, Austin Shaw reported, "They picked up Donnelly on Bondi this morning. Guess he's ruled out."

"Let's not make assumptions," Amanda said. "Serial killers have been known to operate in pairs. If nothing else he's still a possible witness and I want him over here ASAP. Did the search of his flat reveal anything?"

Shaw shook his head. "A few cannabis butts under beds. The flatmate claimed they were all Donnelly's, of course.

"You hear Inspector Ellis on the radio this morning?" Someone piped up.

Several voices chanted in unison. "It is my personal goal to rid this city of filth and corruption . . ."

Amanda lifted inquiring eyebrows. "The Inspector visit the City Art Gallery again?"

There were hoots of laughter. "No, he busted the Sea of Love last night."

It was a spectacular success, she was told. Just after midnight Welch had called in the Vice Squad and told them to carry out the surprise raid. They'd had some kind of tip-off that there were minors turning tricks at the place.

At twelve-thirty, half a dozen Vice Squad officers had closed off all the exits to the Sea of Love bathhouse and adult massage and entered the premises. There were no minors, but the haul included a few grams of coke, all sorts of pills, three

Members of Parliament, a couple of top lawyers, a heart surgeon and the Deputy Mayor!

"Michael Wilson?"Amanda said in disbelief.

"Caught him in a pornomat. Rolling drunk, boxers round his ankles."

"What was he charged with?"

"Nothing. Slept it off downstairs with the rest of them. Released this morning."

Amanda recalled the scene in the carpark. Wilson had spent the night in the slammer at Wellington Central. Her head spun. If Wilson was locked up at the time, who was burning papers in his office?

She glanced at her colleagues. "What time did Welch bring them in?"

"About one-thirty."

Same time as she was down at the garbage dump, slaughtering dogs. Amanda chewed uneasily on her lip. "I'd like to see a copy of that report, Sergeant."

Stifled laughter greeted this request. "Yeah, me too. Bet it'll read juicer than Truth magazine."

In the early afternoon, after digesting the latest spate of Task Force reports, Amanda made an unwilling appearance at the City Council. Several office drones stared. Amanda pretended she didn't notice.

In the elevator, a short man nodded at her and said, "Good afternoon, Inspector Valentine." She smiled vaguely. She didn't know the guy. "You're doing a great job," he informed her. The lift halted at his floor and he held the doors for a moment.

"You've got the public right behind you, Inspector, I want you to know that. It doesn't matter to us that you're an American. Not one little bit."

"Thank you," Amanda said graciously.

When she got to the Mayor's chambers it was worse.

"Inspector Valentine." A junior typist leapt to her feet, eyes doglike. "Can I get you a cup of coffee?"

"Thanks. I'd like that," said Amanda.

"I've brought you these." The girl shyly handed Amanda a bag full of Mars bars. "Since they're your favorite."

Appalled, Amanda took the bag. *Thank you, Debby Daley.*

She had barely been at her desk an hour when the deliveries began. A bunch of flowers, *For your inspiring example to young women* from Zonta. Another from Mayor Perkins himself, *In appreciation.* A cake baked by the tea lady, a voucher from McDonald's for free Big Macs for a month, a curt note from the Chief asking what the hell she thought she was playing at.

Amanda picked up the phone and dialed TVNZ, demanding Debby Daley.

"I'm sorry," the secretary responded like an autowind machine. "Miss Daley is in a meeting."

"Then get her out," Amanda said curtly. "Tell her it's Amanda Valentine."

"Oh, Inspector Valentine. I'll put you right through."

"So you're answering today," Amanda said when she heard Debby's familiar tones.

"Amanda, hi." Debby sounded cool, reserved.

"That program . . ."

"Did you like it?" Uncertainty crept into Debby's voice. "Viewer response has been fantastic."

"I'm happy for you," Amanda said, annoyance bunching in her throat.

There was silence. Amanda could visualize Debby's wounded expression.

"Look, I'm sorry about losing my temper the other night," Debby said in a rush. "It was very sweet of you to send the flowers, even if I did have to take your office girl on a studio tour before she would leave. I'd really like to see you. Please."

"I don't know if that's such a great idea. Besides, I'm not sure how I'll fit you in, what with signing autographs and waving at my fans. Why the hell did you have to make me into a saint for Godsake?"

"But I didn't," Debby denied hotly. "I only asked a few people for their opinions of you and your work. I ran what we got."

"You pumped victims. It was tabloid television."

"You hated it," Debby said dully.

"It so happens I have a few issues around privacy. As in, I need some."

"Oh, come on, Amanda. You work in the public eye. Some part of you must enjoy it."

"Of course I enjoy my job. The fact that the public gets worked up about it is not my doing."

"Nor mine," said Debby. "Can I buy you dinner tonight?"

Amanda grappled with her mixed response to the invitation. She wanted to say no. She wanted to tell Debby Daley to beat it. No one likes to admit they're a prisoner of their own animal nature. "Can we go somewhere I won't get mobbed?" she muttered resignedly.

"Sure." Having got what she wanted, Debby became businesslike. "I heard you found another body at the dump."

"Really?" Amanda said unhelpfully.

Debby laughed again. "Guess I'll just have to wait until you're drunk and indiscreet."

"Don't hold your breath," Amanda told her.

CHAPTER THIRTEEN

Debby was in evening dress, as usual; a red shiny number plucked from the brink of outright indecency by a couple of tiny straps that hitched the bodice across her breasts. The maitre d' hustled them to a secluded table and informed them that fresh Bluff oysters were available today and although Morton Bay Bugs did not appear on the menu, they could be prepared if Miss Daley desired.

"Bugs?" Amanda grimaced.

"My favorite appetizer. They're Australian, a kind of cross between a crab and a lobster. The chef here performs miracles with them with garlic and lemon."

"You eat here often?"

"It's where we put up most of my guests."

"And you grill them over candlelight?"

"Then dissect them on film," Debbie said blandly.

"Don't you ever get sick of poking around in other people's dirty laundry?"

"Don't you?"

The wine steward appeared and Debby startled Amanda by ordering several different bottles after a brief discussion of their choice of courses. Surely the TVNZ entertainment budget didn't stretch that far. The woman was trying to get her drunk, that much was obvious. Well, she'd be disappointed if she expected Amanda to start blathering the names of Garbage Dump Killer suspects the second she'd had a drink or two. Or maybe she thought Amanda would blithely permit herself to be seduced.

Again Amanda reminded herself that Debby's show of sexual interest was merely a cunning ploy; the old honey trap routine. A man would fall for it, but not Amanda Valentine. On her guard, she asked abruptly, "Why don't you do your show as you really are? I mean without the wig and the costumes."

"The costume is part of the show. So is the wig and the pink lipstick. It's an image, a western world icon."

"You mean Barbie? Long on hair, short on brains. You're catering to a male fantasy, Debby. Do you think that really helps women?"

"Women love my show," Debby said. "They love to see men buying that image and falling flat on their faces. They love the glamour."

Amanda wondered whether to Debby that subconsciously translated as they loved her. It was a tempting analysis.

"And it's a part of me, too," Debby said defensively. "I like lovely clothes and fabulous hairstyles. I don't see why I should miss out on all that just because some women don't approve of me."

"But you left it all off the other night when you came around to visit," Amanda observed. "Different audience, different act, I guess."

"Different situation," Debby said quietly. "I mean, don't you change your clothes when you're off duty?"

Amanda frowned. Did she? She became conscious of her Italian weave pants and plain dark jacket. She had a dozen such outfits. Good quality fabrics, practical cut, neutral colors. "No, I don't think I do," she told Debby. "I certainly don't change my personality to go with my outfits."

"Neither do I." Debby looked affronted. "I wish you would accept me the way I am." Her bottom lip gave a convincing tremble. "I'd really like us to get to know each other."

It was the same well-worn record; I just want to be your friend . . . Maybe it was time to call Debby's bluff, Amanda thought, teach her not to mess with the big girls.

They sat in silence as a waiter arranged Amanda's appetizer, Bluff oysters in the half shell on a bed of ice. Debby was only having one course. The camera showed up every bulge, she said.

Amanda stared down at her oysters and smiled tenderly. This was going to be a religious experience. With a purposeful jab, she speared the first of the plump mollusks and examined its delicate folds. Then she extended it across the table to brush Debby's startled lips. Debby blushed profusely and her eyes widened with shock. Amanda met them squarely, intently.

"Have an oyster," she invited.

Debby opened her mouth to receive it. She looked dazed.

Amanda swallowed several of the slippery things in quick succession, observing, "Juicy, aren't they?"

Debby was chewing hers like she was eating cardboard. Wild color had spread down her face to her throat.

"You're looking very flushed,"Amanda noted casually.

Debby's hands fluttered to her cheeks then she pulled them hastily away and made a show of rearranging her napkin. "It's quite warm in here, isn't it?"

Amanda squeezed a little lemon on the few shellfish remaining and offered Debby another.

Debby shook her head. She was taking short shallow gulps of air. "It's a real heat wave," she started chattering. "The hottest January since the war. It's never been so humid in Wellington. No rain, just muggy. I've hardly slept a wink this week. I just don't know what to do with myself."

Amanda finished her last oyster and licked the aftertaste off her lips. "Have you tried masturbating," she said placidly.

Debby gasped, braved a quick uncertain look at Amanda, then stared somewhat desperately toward the kitchen.

As though on cue, a waiter materialized and cleared Amanda's place. For a wicked moment Amanda toyed with the idea of ordering another dozen oysters, but it seemed almost unsporting. She already had Debby on the run. For once the other woman seemed bereft of speech.

Amanda helped her out. "The way I see it, if you're lying there all hot and sticky and restless, you might as well make the most of it."

"By masturbating?" Debby asked weakly.

"Sure." Amanda shrugged.

Debby gulped down some wine, studied her polished fingertips. The nails were short and neatly filed, marginal for a bimbo. "I prefer company myself," she said in a tight little voice.

We'll see, Amanda thought with grim satisfaction.

The waiter served their main courses. Debby was binging on diet food: grilled fish, multiple salads, no dressing; Amanda had ordered venison on a bed of wild rice and pine nuts, topped with tamarillos in brandy. She hoped there'd be room for dessert.

"Company can be pleasant," she conceded after a couple of mouthfuls, "but so often it's unreliable."

Debby paused between segments of melon. "Unreliable? What do you mean?"

"Disappointing," Amanda mused. "You know how it is. You take someone home, you're aroused, maybe fantasizing. You get their clothes off and suddenly they need to floss their teeth. They scream when you show them your sex toys. They think a blindfold is

S/M." She dropped her voice. "They want the lights out for oral sex."

Debby had stopped eating entirely. She seemed transfixed. Amanda wondered if she'd overdone the scare tactics. She could almost see the headlines: *Handcuffs Double As Sex Aid, Says Deviant Detective.*

Debby looked on the verge of tears again. Amanda dredged up a phoney laugh. "Only joking."

Debby forced a wobbly smile and began fidgeting with the tiny straps that held up her red satin bodice. She looked like a small animal paralyzed in the glare of oncoming headlights.

Suddenly Amanda felt boorish and guilty.

They ate in taut silence for a few minutes, Amanda flagellating herself for overplaying her hand.

Then Debby burst out, "Come home with me tonight. I want to make love with you. We can have the lights on if you want."

Amanda choked on a pine nut. A waiter scuttled over with fresh water and a small plate of bread cubes.

"I'm not a dull person," Debby insisted. "I enjoy trying new things. You can even tie me up if you want."

Amanda's palms began to sweat. Christ. Debby was into bondage. That was all she needed.

"Don't you fancy me at all?" Debby was pleading.

Their coffee arrived. Amanda tried not to make a grab for her cup before the waiter had finished groveling.

"I fancy you," she admitted quietly.

"Then what's the problem? I'm not the possessive type. I don't want to get married or anything."

"It's me. I'm the problem. I use women, Debby. I've been doing that for a long time. I play 'round, I don't get involved and my job comes first. Always." Amanda drained her glass. "I don't want to see you hurt."

"Ever thought about getting an ego reduction?" Debby inquired sarcastically. "C'mon, for God's sake. I'm not asking you to get involved. We could have fun. No strings attached. If you want kinky sex, we can have kinky sex."

"I do not want kinky sex." Amanda raised her voice. A couple of diners turned around.

Debby's big blue eyes sparkled boldly across the table at her. "Why don't we discuss this at my place?"

Amanda sighed. A beautiful woman was offering her a good time, no complications, and she was declining. Time to visit the shrink. What was the harm in a one-night stand? It sure beat another steamy week of unrequited lust. The whole deal would probably be an anticlimax and they could cheerfully say goodbye and never see each other again. Pigs could fly.

It was academic anyway. The sordid truth was she had the hots for Debby Daley and sooner or later lust was going to overtake her common sense. The way she was feeling right now, sooner seemed like a good idea.

"Okay," she said, stomach sinking. "But it had better be my place. In case I'm called out."

* * * * *

Amanda closed the door and bolted it. She walked Debby through the place so she knew where the bathroom was.

"Can I get you a drink?" she asked.

Debby shook her head. "I'd like to take a shower."

"Help yourself."

"You can join me if you like."

Amanda's throat felt dry and her pulse hammered. She followed Debby into the bathroom and tried to act as if she took showers with casual lovers all the time. She hoped Debby wasn't expecting *9-1/2 weeks* or anything.

The other woman seemed remarkably blasé. Prepared, it seemed, for anything, she pulled a toothbrush from a little bag she'd brought in and placed it on the bathroom vanity, along with a comb and some Obsession perfume. Tossing her wig down beside the rest of her gear, she turned to Amanda and asked, "Can you unzip me?"

Amanda obliged and felt her stomach drop as Debby stepped out of the shiny dress. She had on underwear that Amanda had seen in glossy magazines but never thought anyone except drag queens actually wore. It was satin and stretch lace. Deep burgundy with little bows, all matching — strapless bra, panties, suspender belt. Amanda reflected on her own sensible white cotton gear and cringed.

Inside the exotic undies Debby Daley's body was exactly as Amanda had imagined it, maybe even better. She wasn't thin. She was all curves, her flesh smooth and lightly tanned. Her breasts were very full and her dark nipples showed beneath the lacy bra.

She removed her frillies with orderly movements and turned on the shower. There was no coyness about her nudity, nothing tense or deliberately provocative in her common sense undressing. Yet everything about her was unbearably erotic. The dark hair clinging damply to her head, the downward stroke of her long fingers as she rolled her stockings off, the two small dimples like thumbprints at the base of her spine.

Amanda doggedly removed her own clothes and was suddenly conscious of Debby's eyes on her, bright with candid interest. Her flesh goosebumped and she felt too naked in the harsh light. It was like a goddamned locker room.

"Great shower," said Debby impersonally. "Come on in."

Amanda drew a breath and did just that.

Debby passed her the soap, tilting her face to the blast of the water. Her hair was slick and black against her head and her lashes were spangled with tiny droplets. Amanda stared at her neck and wanted to kiss it.

"Here, let me." Debby took the soap back again and reached around Amanda to do her back. Her fingers were firm and confident, her breasts brushed Amanda's, their faces touched, their thighs and bellies connected.

"That feels good," Amanda said, struggling to catch her breath.

"You're very muscular. I guess you work out."

Amanda nodded. "I have to keep fit. Part of the job." Debby's hands had worked their way down to cup her buttocks. She had a flooding sensation in her groin.

"Stamina is so important." Debby licked some of the water from around Amanda's mouth and kept licking.

Amanda tightened her arms, locking Debby close. Her mouth tasted sweet and hot. Amanda left it briefly to kiss her neck and shoulders, then her breasts. Debby sighed, eyes closed, and Amanda was struck by her beauty, the vulnerable softness of her mouth, the delicate hollows of her shoulders. She was wet and open and Amanda slid a finger slowly back and forth between her thighs until, shaking, Debby buried her face in Amanda's shoulder.

They were still damp when they tumbled into bed, and their lovemaking was at first hot and passionate, the wild, abandoned fulfillment of pent up desire. Later it became tender and unhurried, the sense-luscious expedition of new lovers discovering one another.

When eventually they fell asleep, it was locked together, caught between exhausted kisses.

CHAPTER FOURTEEN

Amanda could hardly believe her bad luck when her bleeper sounded. Dragging herself upright, she flicked on the bedside lamp and stretched limbs heavy with the aftermath of passion. For a split second she was startled to see a dark head on the pillow next to her. Then she relaxed and pushed the sweaty bedclothes to one side.

As she phoned in, she watched Debby. She was comatose; flat on her back and emitting occasional satisfied moans. Amanda fought off a powerful urge to get back into bed and climb all over her.

It was a homicide call. Jockeying her brain into gear, Amanda scribbled the address and gathered together some clothes. For a furtive moment, she stared down at Debby and a flood of images played across her mind. She remembered the silky smooth feel of her, the uninhibited pleasure Debby took in her body, the astounding sensations she had aroused.

Just looking at her, Amanda felt like one of Pavlov's dogs. Where the hell had Debby learned to make love like that? Who else did she go to bed with? All of a sudden the room seemed smothering, and Amanda stalked hastily out the door. What was it to her who Debby Daley had sex with? They weren't going to do this again anyway. Debby was a fling, a spot of judicious stress relief.

She turned on the shower and could hardly bear to get in alone. She looked at her face in the mirror. Her hair was tousled, her eyes were heavy and knowing, and her mouth looked slightly swollen. There was something else too, something ancient and fragile. Amanda turned away, not wanting to see it.

Chris Clarke was dead. Amanda felt winded, responsible — as if, having talked to the man, she should somehow have foreseen his impending death and prevented it.

She stalked up the familiar curved slate driveway, visually sweeping the environs for anything that didn't quite mesh. Her gaze halted abruptly, arrested by an impression in the velvety lawn ahead of her. It swung off the driveway then back onto it, leaving a single distinct arc on the lawn. Amanda approached the mark, knelt and examined the flattened grass. The mark felt dry, obviously not brand new. A faint tire track. Someone had driven away in a big hurry.

The air-conditioned interior of the house contrasted sharply with the oppressive heat of the night. Passing a uniformed Constable, Amanda entered the scene of the crime.

The room was spacious, expensive art prints dotting the walls, recessed lighting pouring a gentle glow over soft modern furnishings. On the far side, French doors opened out onto floodlit decking and an olympic-size swimming pool.

Several opulent sofas were aesthetically arranged in the center of the room, and slumped in one of these was Chris Clarke. He was white and staring, surrounded by a black pool of congealed blood. Spotlit in the fierce beams of the police photographer's arc-lights, he looked like the central performer in some macabre stage production.

A knot of people stood a few paces away from the body. Amanda identified Chief Pathologist Moira McDougall, David Wong, the police photographer, and Gordon Webley, a CIB Detective Sergeant often used as a scenes of crime officer. Standing over them, like a bird of prey, was Bob Welch.

"Inspector." Amanda approached him with a controlled expression. "Good of you to drop by."

He returned a curt nod.

"I understand you are in the middle of a surveillance operation. I won't keep you."

Welch surveyed her with pallid indifference. "This is my case, Valentine." He waved a small plastic bag. "Cocaine," he explained, mouth twitching. "We've had our eye on Clarke for some time now."

Amanda bit back a retort and allowed her gaze to travel over Clarke again. He was in casual clothes. A single glass of wine sat half-finished on the low table in front of him. A bottle next to it had a couple of inches left in the bottom. A second empty bottle lay on its side beneath the little table. There was no sign of any struggle.

Amanda made a mental note to check his blood/alcohol levels with McDougall. If Chris Clarke had been drinking alone he must have been a write-off when he was killed. It seemed odd that he would have been reading a fifty-page legal document in that state, she thought, noticing the blood-spattered contract opened flat on the floor at his feet.

"How long has he been dead?" she asked Moira McDougall.

With a stoic air, the Pathologist switched off her pocket tape recorder. Moira was a small, spare woman in her late forties. Her light brown hair was short and neatly combed and she studied the world from behind gold-rimmed specs which she constantly adjusted during conversation. Like many women who make it to the top of their professions, she had a reputation for being cold and unapproachable. In Moira's own words, she wasn't paid to suffer fools and she had no intention of doing so.

She seemed releived to see Amanda, commenting, "He's been dead around twenty-four hours. Certainly the wine's a day old."

At which point Welch arrogantly butted in. "Valentine will be free to read the report."

"I have all but finished at the Mayor's Office, Bob," Amanda said sharply. "So there won't be any need for you to take over this inquiry. I appreciate your interest from a narcotics perspective and I'll keep you informed of developments. I'll give the Chief a call now and discuss it with him."

"That won't be necessary." Welch held his ground without blinking. "I've already spoken to the Chief. Given your slow progress on the Garbage Dump Killer inquiry, he's assigned the case to me."

What! "We'll see about that," Amanda snapped. This was the last straw, she thought, seething. She was being blatantly sidelined, her career torpedoed. Why? Because she was a woman, an easy target? Had she been set up to fail in order to provide justification for a promotion system that was still heavily loaded in favor of men?

"I hear you found some more remains," Welch remarked with a hint of mockery. "And that dog, of course. Shot dead only a few feet away. Extraordinary business. Got a suspect yet?"

The taunt was so pointed that even Moira McDougall paused in her meticulous sampling of fibers to frown at Welch.

He wanted her to fail, Amanda realized with sickening clarity. The Garbage Dump case was the kind that could make or break a career, and this man, her colleague, was hoping for the latter. She felt like punching his teeth in.

Her voice shook with rage as she responded, "No, we don't have a suspect, Bob. But we do have a witness!"

Damn, she thought, the second she had uttered the half-truth. She was going to have egg all over her face if Donnelly didn't know a thing and his car had been stolen.

Welch was staring, his disbelief palpable. Amanda watched the color draining from his face and felt no remorse. Let him think she was about to solve the case! Let him sweat imagining the slavish press hanging on her every word, the letter of commendation from the Minister of Police . . .

Hard-eyed, she surveyed the room, committing it to memory. Then with a nod at McDougall, she turned on her heel. As she marched through the double doors, she paused, momentarily startled. Just inside the doorway was a huge floral arrangement. Beneath it a shower of tiny white flower heads had fallen. Gypsophylla.

Amanda returned home at 3:00 AM to the disconcerting sight of Debby wearing a borrowed dressing gown and rattling about in her kitchen cupboards.

"Hi!" Debby greeted her with a frank smile and stretched out her arms. "Do you normally vanish straight after lovemaking, or have I got bad breath?"

"I'm sorry," Amanda began. "I got called out —"

Debby put her fingers briefly to Amanda's lips, then kissed her very thoroughly. "I'm only teasing." She drew back to stare inquiringly into Amanda's eyes. "You look upset."

Heaving a sigh, Amanda allowed her hands to drop to the small of Debby's back. How much should she tell Debby? Nothing, her common sense dictated. With a pang of guilt, she moved out of Debby's arms and poured each of them a coffee.

"Shall I run you a bath?" Debby offered.

Amanda shook her head. Watching Debby sip coffee, she felt like kicking herself. It was Debby who had alerted her to Clarke in the first place. If only Amanda had taken her more seriously. If only she had listened. Instead she had been tripped up by her own prejudices, patronizing the "bimbo" she'd decided Debby was.

"Debby," she said circumspectly, "about Chris Clarke . . ."

Debby's eyes swung to her face, alert and inquiring. "Have you found out something about him?"

"In a manner of speaking."

Amanda felt discomforted by Debby's piercing regard. Debby was the media, she told herself. The fact that they'd gone to bed together changed nothing. But meeting those aquamarine eyes, Amanda was alarmingly conscious of her common sense evaporating.

"Chris Clarke's dead," she said tonelessly. "Murdered."

Debby lowered her coffee mug to the table with a thud. "Murdered! When?"

"Wednesday. But his body was found tonight."

"So that's where you were. Do you know who did it?"

"Not yet."

"Wow." Debby gazed into space. Almost inaudibly, she said, "That's so weird."

Amanda observed her closely. "What do you mean?"

"Oh ... nothing really. Just an odd coincidence." Her eyes sought out Amanda's, apparently seeking assurance that Amanda wasn't merely humoring her.

"Tell me about it." Amanda was suddenly very conscious of the possible value of Debby's observations.

"I've been asking around ..." Debby said. "I talked to this guy who was once on my show. He's a bouncer at *Ask The Angels* — the nightclub."

"You saw Clarke there?"

"I was following him ..."

"You were what!" Amanda made a concerted effort to keep the anger out of her tone. While she had been twiddling her thumbs, Debby Daley had been tailing the prime suspect in the Jezebel beating, a man who was at the very least a nasty small-time villain and at worst a ruthless drug boss. What if he'd caught her in the act?

"You said you wanted something concrete," Debby responded defensively. "He hung around the clubs all the time. So I talked to Sonny ..."

"The bouncer?"

Debby frowned at the cross-check. "Yes, the bouncer. He knew Chris Clarke, and — this is the weird bit — he warned me to stay away from him. He said something about people disappearing."

"Disappearing?" Amanda's pulse gave a speed wobble. "Okay," she said briskly. "Let's start again. What did this Sonny say — can you remember his exact words?"

"That's easy." Debby smiled, obviously pleased with herself. "I wrote it all down."

She wrote it down. Reporters did, Amanda reminded herself with heavy cynicism. They had that in common with cops.

Debby was flicking methodically through a shorthand pad. "Here it is." She waved a page of hieroglyphics in front of Amanda, demanding with thinly disguised amusement, "Want me to translate?"

Amanda nodded. Had her dismay been that obvious? She got the distinct impression Debby was chalking up mileage out of this. Good luck to her, she thought morosely. She deserved it.

"This is what he said." Debby inserted suitable melodrama. *"He's one heavy customer. You wanna keep outta his face, Debby.* I asked him what he meant — I said Clarke wanted a date. *Don't even think about it. Life's too short, babe. I'll tell you something about our Christopher. Word around here is his friends have a habit of disappearing . . . know what I'm saying?"*

"That's it?"

Debby closed the pad and lifted serious eyes. "I figured disappear really meant die. That's why it felt weird when you told me about Chris Clarke. I mean, he's the one who got murdered, after all."

"Do you have any idea who these 'friends' of Clarke are?" Amanda asked.

"No. Sonny didn't tell me any more. You think one of them might have done it?"

"Most victims are killed by someone they know."

Debby seemed hesitant all of a sudden. "I didn't say anything before, because . . ."

"You knew I wouldn't listen," Amanda completed dryly.

Debby looked at the floor. "I'm sorry . . ."

"No. I am," Amanda said. "I owe you an apology —"

"Don't." Debby reached for Amanda's hand and lifted it to her mouth, nibbling the finger ends. "I like it better when you're tough . . ."

"Really?"

Debby stood. The thin dressing gown slid tantalizing off one shoulder then the other. Then it was on the floor and Debby was stepping out of it. Naked, she smiled.

Amanda told herself she had better things to do than follow Debby Daley into the bedroom, but somehow that didn't seem to stop her. As Debby divested her of her clothes, she reminded herself that she was in full control of the situation. But when Debby's arms closed around her, she found she no longer wanted to be.

A few exhausting hours later, Amanda labored her way along Manners Street, certain her debauchery was written all over her face.

It was still the summer vacation. The footpaths were crowded with school kids stuffing ice creams, spitting gum and elbowing their mates. Faded mothers pushed strollers two abreast, complaining about the heat and the lousy manners of bus drivers. Fat men in mustard shorts crowded the donut cart and groups of youths, hostage to their hormones, lurked in doorways yelling out to passing schoolgirls.

Every shop was having a sale, forlorn Christmas stock marked down to clear. Amanda bought Debby a box of liqueur chocolates for half price, then felt cheap and ate them herself. By the time she reached the cafe, she felt pleasantly sick.

Joe was already dug in with a Coke and pizza. Amanda procured a murky liquid the management was passing off as coffee and joined him. "I suppose you've heard," she said.

"About Clarke?" Joe grimaced. "Welch reckons he'll have an arrest within forty-eight hours."

Amanda rolled her eyes. "Oh, swell."

"What's going on?" Joe said bluntly. "The guy's all over your patch, kid."

"Jesus. Don't I know it!" She shook her head. "This whole business is starting to feel like a set-up."

"Talk to the Chief."

Amanda gave a harsh laugh. "You think that'll make a difference? It's the Chief who's giving Welch my cases. It's the Chief who dropped me into this Council thing."

Joe gave her a cryptic look. "I don't want to hear this."

"Someone's gunning for me, Joe," she said, cradling her head. "And I don't understand why."

Joe was silent, his expression brooding. "Okay," he said softly. "Chill out a moment. I'll get some more coffee."

Amanda watched him squeeze past the crowded tables and understood suddenly how much she depended on him. You could do that with friends, she supposed. *But not with lovers,* came a tiny familiar message from her subconscious. For the first time in five years, Amanda paused to examine that assumption. Was it really true?

Joe dragged out his chair and subsided into it, depositing two cups on the table. "I've been thinking." He returned to his pizza. "Those papers you found in the Deputy Mayor's office. They connect Wilson and Clarke, right?"

Amanda nodded.

"So what say Wilson's up to his ears in some kind of scam with Clarke and he wants out ... He's worried about getting caught. The guy wants to be Mayor, right?"

"Go on." Abruptly Amanda recalled that overheard phone call, Wilson saying: *I want out too, buddy ... Okay, I'll talk to him.*

Joe was setting out a theory. "So he offs Clarke and nips up to his office to get rid of incriminating evidence."

"Joe. Clarke was killed sometime between twelve and two. The papers in Wilson's office were most likely burnt between two and three. Wilson was at the Sea of Love getting arrested at the time. The report says they busted the place at twelve-thirty and found him blotto. Some hooker reckons she did him an hour before then. They loaded him into a van and he was checked into the overnight cells at one-thirty. From where I'm standing, that's a crash-hot alibi."

Joe scratched his head.

"We're trying to adapt facts to fit a theory," Amanda said. "And they don't."

"So find another theory. Leaving aside the value judgments."

"I saw Wilson leaving the station the morning after the bust," Amanda said. "He was in the parking lot with Bob Welch." She recalled the two men standing in the carpark, Welch touching Wilson's shoulder, watching him walk away, then glaring at her. "There was something odd about it."

"Odd?"

"They looked like friends . . . the way they were talking. It looked private . . ."

Joe gave her the *You need a holiday* stare. Again that phone call hovered in the background of her mind. *I want out too, buddy.*

Who was the "buddy" Wilson was talking to? Who had arranged an unscheduled bust the night Chris Clarke was killed, and had also managed to get himself assigned to the case?

"Joe," Amanda said. "I have a theory."

"Makes a nice change from a hunch," her stalwart colleague replied.

"There's something that connects the murder scene to Wilson's office."

"Apart from those papers?"

"There was this little white flower . . ."

Joe shook his head. "Try telling that to a jury."

At the Station, Austin Shaw was waiting in an interview room with their potential witness.

Bruce Donnelly was slim and darkly tanned, well presented for a beach bum. Somehow he didn't come across as half of a deadly duo. He was making a poor job of hiding something.

In November he'd advertised his car for sale, he said. "I needed the bread."

"So your car was sold?"

"Basically, yes." He frowned as though confronted with an elaborate Chinese puzzle. "In the final analysis ... you could say it was sold."

"The vehicle is still registered under your name," Amanda commented, letting him see she found this very odd.

Another frown. "So, the guy didn't switch the papers over." A shrug. "Yeah, well I'm not into that bureaucratic shit either."

"Can you give us the name of the person who purchased your car, Mr. Donnelly?"

"Hey. Call me Bruce, okay? This Mr. Donnelly stuff makes me feel old."

"The name?"

"Oh, yeah. Right." He squinted at the ceiling. "I wrote it somewhere ..."

"Were you paid by check?"

"No. Er ..."

"Mr. Donnelly ... Bruce. We are investigating a serious crime. Your car is involved. We need as much information as you can give us."

"A serious crime?" He swallowed hard, glanced from Amanda to Shaw, apparently seeking reassurance. "Do you think I should get a lawyer?" he asked.

"That's up to you," Amanda said patiently. "At this point you're not charged with anything."

"Oh." He sat up straighter. "No. Hey, it's okay. This is important, right. Is it like . . . a murder?"

"Why do you ask?"

Donnelly flushed. "Well . . . Man, that's heavy." He paused, a slow realization dawning. "Jesus! You don't think . . . Shit!"

"Is there something you'd like to tell us, Bruce?"

Amanda signaled Shaw with a slight nod. Shaw said earnestly, "Are you sure you understand your rights, Bruce? Would you like me to read them again?"

"No! Man, this is giving me the shits. I haven't done anything." His eyes were begging them for belief. "Look," he blurted. "What say, hypothetically, someone innocent gets tangled up in this kind of trip and they've done . . . like some minor thing. So . . . like they blow it if they tell you what you want . . ."

Sonny, we don't care if you've got a dope plant growing in your bedroom, Amanda thought wearily.

"Bruce, we need your help." Shaw was at his best making a pitch for truth, justice and the triumph of decency over a guilty conscience. "We can't make hollow promises about how we will use the information you give us. But lives are at risk, Bruce. You could make a difference."

Donnelly swallowed. "It's the Garbage Dump Killer, right?" When Amanda and Shaw were silent, he went on. "Fuck, man. I could have met the guy. I could have . . ."

Amanda surveyed his pale face and said softly, "Please try and remember every detail, Bruce. Sometimes the little things are infinitely the most important."

He grinned, a trace of color returning to his cheeks. "Sherlock Holmes."

Amanda grinned back. "Did you say you were an artist, Bruce?"

CHAPTER FIFTEEN

In a state of shock, Amanda left the station.

After two hours, three Fosters and a good deal of positive reinforcement, Bruce Donnelly had finally produced a stunning likeness of the Deputy Mayor himself.

Austin had approached the matter with commendable self-restraint. "He's a dope freak," he had told Amanda. "He probably saw twenty thousand of Wilson's election posters on the ride in from the airport."

"He seemed pretty adamant that this was the guy who gave him two hundred cash and an ounce of green in exchange for the car."

"Does that sound like something the Deputy Mayor would do?"

"God knows," Amanda had sighed. "But I'm going to talk to the guy. Let's not flaunt the sketch yet."

It was a logical impossibility, she convinced herself as she drove home. Setting aside the small matter of his alibi, Wilson was still her chief suspect in the Clarke killing. Somehow he had been at Clarke's house around midnight, killed the guy, gathered a few little white flowers as he left, driven to his office and burned those papers. Between times he had managed to be picked up at the Sea of Love and taken downtown, establishing a perfect alibi.

Unwise as it was to make assumptions until all the data was gathered, it was stretching credibility to imagine him down at the dump, getting rid of "Boris's" frozen head as well. Besides, Michael Wilson didn't look like the owner of size twelve feet.

Before she called on Wilson that afternoon, she needed to change her clothes, she decided. Basic psychology. You don't question a prime suspect when you're feeling low caliber and unwashed, and wearing a sticky shirt.

She dumped her briefcase in the hallway and wandered into the kitchen. Her fridge hummed alluringly. She contemplated its congested shelves, frowned, then glanced uncertainly around her living area. The curtains were drawn, the place was silent.

She paced into the sitting room, sniffed the air, gazed down at the Indian cotton pillows on her sofa, stuck her finger into the dirt around a potted plant. The cat flap banged and Madam made an entrance in full eloquent voice.

Amanda squatted to stroke the little cat, picked up her bag and trudged upstairs into her bedroom. In the hallway she caught a waft of familiar scent. She wracked her brains. It wasn't her own Ann Klein, or Debby's Obsession. It wasn't Mrs. Thompson's toilet cleaner or the scented kitty litter.

Dropping her bag on her bed, she unbuttoned her jacket, pulled and checked her gun, and, holding it alongside her thigh, slipped noiselessly into the hallway.

The grandfather clock ticked steadily, a tap dripped in the bathroom. A curtain was flapping beyond the closed door of the guestroom . . .

Gun braced, Amanda kicked open the door.

Sitting on the bed, a wig in one hand and a mascara wand in the other, was a man wearing lipstick and foundation garments.

"Jezebel!" Amanda hissed.

"So what could I do, honey?" Jezebel sighed over coffee a half hour later.

"You discharged yourself?"

"Heavens, no. You think those girls would let me outta that place?" Jezebel rolled her eyes, mimicking. "Ve haf our orters, Miss Matenka."

Mouth twitching, Amanda poured more coffee, liberally adding brandy to Jezebel's. She regarded her visitor with somber eyes. Jezebel hadn't had her stitches out yet, but the swelling was gradually going down and makeup covered much of her bruising.

"Can you repeat exactly what Ricky said?" Amanda asked.

"He was real scared."

"Jezebel . . ."

"All right. Okay. So, he comes into the hospital real late."

"This is last night?"

Jezebel nodded. "He says Clarke's dead and he's gotta blow this place. He gives me money and tells me to wise up an' get out too. He was *real* scared."

"Jezebel, did Ricky kill Chris Clarke?"

Jezebel looked indignant. "Of course not! Lovie, I know he didn't do that."

"What makes you so sure?"

Jezebel hesitated, her mascaraed lashes drooping. "That's my boy," she said huskily. "My son. I know he'd never do nothing like that."

Amanda gaped. Her son? Her mind reeled as a bunch of stray pieces slotted into place. No wonder Jezebel seemed to have her loyalties confused. No wonder she'd been so twitchy discussing Hippolyte. Her son . . .

Amanda pushed her fingers wearily into her hair. Motive. Clarke was responsible for Jezebel's beating. And if Ricky was her son . . . "How do you know he didn't do it, Jezebel?"

"I know my boy."

Amanda lifted a Pink Triangle magazine off her cabinet and fanned herself reflectively. She thought about that single tire track swerving across Clarke's lawn. Had Ricky paid Clarke a visit on Thursday, found him dead and scarpered with whatever money he could lay his hands on? Or was Jezebel a poor judge of her offspring's character and Hippolyte was capable of murder after all?

"Jezebel. Do you know who killed Chris Clarke?"

"No idea. That boy sure did know how to win friends and influence people."

Amanda studied her visitor, knowing in her gut that Jezebel still hadn't told her everything. She leaned forward. "Jezebel. You're holding out on me. I have to know about you and Chris Clarke. I want the truth this time."

Jezebel shook her head. "Forget it, lovie. The scum's dead anyway ..."

"He can't hurt you any more, huh?"

Jezebel flashed haunted eyes at her.

"You know what I think," Amanda said in her toughest voice. "I think you know who killed Chris Clarke."

"I don't! I got no idea who done it."

Amanda stood up, gazing pitilessly at the lavishly clad figure. "Someone will think you do, Jezebel. And they'll come after you. A shame," she added, shrugging, "but there's nothing I can do about it. You better go home."

Jezebel went pale under her Malibu bronze foundation cream. "Sweet Jesus. You throwing me out, honey?"

"Well, you can't stay here. What would your customers think?"

Jezebel fidgeted tearfully with an earring. "I'll tell you the truth, doll. I got nowhere to go. Julie or one of the others would put me up for a while but you know what happens when you share. Nothing is sacred. I get real fed up with other girls using my stuff. It's better if I live alone."

"I'm only a phone call away." That hadn't helped last time, Amanda reminded herself.

Jezebel burst into tears. "I can't go back home. Hippo said so. I wish I never went to that place," she sobbed. "White limousine ..."

Amanda opened the door. "Looks like we better bring Ricky in. You'll probably be called as a witness ..."

Jezebel gasped.

"Of course I'm not saying he did it ... for certain ... But there's a lot of circumstantial evidence."

"Circumstantial evidence! Get a brain transplant, doll. They found my friend Neil dead in some cell too ... that mean the police killed him?"

"Jezebel!"

"Okay. All right." Jezebel got to her feet with a toss of her wig. "I'll go fetch something for you, Miss Valentine, but you gotta make me a promise."

"What?"

"When they bury me you see to it I'm in my emrall' green evening dress with the pink sequin shoes. Don't you let them put me in my casket in boy drag."

"Jezebel," Amanda said fiercely, "there isn't going to be any funeral. Just go get whatever it is you've got, for Chrissakes."

Reining in her temper, she checked the door and pulled the curtains closed.

Jezebel returned and, with an injured sniff, passed Amanda a black ledger book.

It was crammed full of accounting records. Dates, payments, names and job descriptions. Like any sensible businessperson, Chris Clarke had kept a detailed record of every transaction he made, a record which, no doubt, doubled as an insurance policy should any of his contacts attempt to double-cross him.

Amanda took a deep steadying breath. "Do you realize why this is important?"

"Well, sure, doll. I can read."

Amanda flicked to the back of the book. There was a list of names with ticks and crosses beside them. Most of them Amanda recognized. Police, Customs Officials. Men whose careers would be ruined if the notebook was made public.

"I thought the scum would pay something to get it back."

"And you weren't going to tell me about this, were you? What was the plan, Jezebel? Did you think you could put the squeeze on someone else as well?"

"I already did." Jezebel seized the book and pointed at a name.

Michael Wilson.

There was a large Volvo station wagon parked in front of the Wilson's Lower Hutt residence. The place was a celebration of kitsch, the product of an unhappy marriage between new money and poor taste. The front entrance of this distressed masterpiece featured vast slabs of white marble, black marble pillars, glass bricks and ornamental lions.

Amanda fed her name into an intercom and the door was opened by a jumpy-looking Filipino woman who told her to wait in the hallway. Obediently, she occupied a silly triangular chrome chair. On the opposite wall a huge fiber optics fountain constantly changed color. Amanda could feel her jaw dropping as she took it all in.

A woman appeared and the hallway was suddenly redolent with the oversweet fragrance of Estée Lauder Youth Dew. The woman was small and dainty, expensively dressed. Expert makeup added color to her sallow complexion and fullness to a thin, disappointed mouth.

She surveyed Amanda with insipid hazel eyes. In a sugary voice, she announced, "I'm Harriet Wilson. You're here to see my husband, I believe."

Amanda offered her ID along with her most guileless smile. "That's correct, Mrs. Wilson. I'm Detective Inspector Amanda Valentine."

"How do you do, Inspector Valentine," Harriet said. "My husband has spoken highly of you."

Knowing she was expected to find this flattering, Amanda smiled faintly. "Is Mr. Wilson here?"

Harriet Wilson flicked a darting look at the tiny gold watch on her wrist. "No. But I'm expecting him shortly. Would you care for a drink or perhaps some coffee while you wait?"

Opting for coffee, Amanda followed her hostess into a sitting room with walls of white marble.

"What an atmospheric room," she remarked when they were seated. "Do you do your own designing, Mrs. Wilson?"

The red mouth stretched primly around small, even teeth. "I do, as a matter of fact."

"The marble is very exciting," Amanda lied.

Mrs. Wilson modestly rearranged her skirt. "Do you really like it?"

Amanda was reminded fleetingly of Debby after lovemaking. *Did you really like it? ... Was I really okay?* Some women needed this constant reassurance. Thin, tense Harriet Wilson appeared to be hanging on her every word.

"I think it's very powerful." Amanda warmed to her theme. "Classical ... understated. Tell me, how did you get those pictures up there? Not nails, surely."

Mrs. Wilson put one hand to her mouth as though stifling a giggle. "Actually," she leaned forward, *sotto voce,* "we glued them."

Amanda fought to control almost hysterical laughter. Works by several major Australian and New Zealand artists were grouped around the room. Valuable, irreplaceable paintings, and the Wilsons had glued them to the walls.

"We got the idea from McDonald's," Mrs. Wilson added without missing a beat.

Amanda smelled coffee and watched the Filipino maid set it out. After the woman had gone, Mrs. Wilson drew Amanda's attention to a small spill. "I'm still training her," she said with a slight sniff. "You have to be firm with them."

Oh sure, just like dogs. *Maid obedience ...* Amanda told herself not to blow it. She sipped her coffee and checked the time. "I hope I'm not holding you up, Mrs. Wilson."

"It's my pleasure, Inspector." Harriet Wilson patted her well-sprayed blonde curls, and crossed, then uncrossed her legs. "It's not often I have the chance to talk to a famous detective." She gave a small self-deprecating laugh.

Amanda cleared her throat modestly. "It's just a job, Mrs. Wilson."

"Please call me Harriet." Her companion fluttered. "All the same, it must be very exciting."

Perceiving that Harriet Wilson was committed to her topic, Amanda resorted to the standard PR spiel. "It's mostly plod, I'm afraid. Miles of paperwork, plenty of frustration. And I'm no star. I'm just one of a team."

"Are you close to catching the Garbage Dump Killer yet? You know what I think?" Harriet lowered her voice to a stage whisper. "I think he kills them at home then hides the pieces in his rubbish and waits for the garbage truck to come along and take it all away."

You, and ninety callers a day. "That's certainly one theory, Harriet," Amanda said sagely.

"Are they ... you know ... sex murders? It doesn't say in the papers."

"I'm afraid I'm not at liberty to answer that."

"Of course. Silly me. Anyway, I know you're going to catch him. Michael says you're one smart lady."

"I'm flattered." Amanda smiled. Just wolfishly enough so the other woman shifted in her seat. "Your husband is very dedicated, isn't he?" she murmured.

"Oh, yes. Mikey just slaves for the City."

"And he's not even Mayor."

For a split second, anger pinched Harriet's small oval face. "That may change." Her voice rose a key or two, cracking slightly.

"You mean in the next elections?"

"Well, it was a close thing last time." Open resentment darkened the vacuous hazel eyes to near green. "Just a few hundred votes in fact."

"So it could go either way," Amanda observed. "All depends on the media, I suppose."

"What do you mean?"

"Publicity. It's the same back home. A hint of scandal and . . ." She ran a graphic finger across her throat.

Flinching, Harriet glanced at her watch, and said in a strained voice, "Oh, dear. Mikey is late. I wonder what's keeping him."

Amanda thought about the Sea of Love and wondered how many nights Harriet Wilson had spent peering anxiously at the door and going to bed alone. "Perhaps you can help me," she said sweetly. "I need to ask both you and your husband a few routine questions in relation to a murder we're investigating."

"Murder?" Harriet's eyes were glassy again.

"Yes. Would you mind telling me what you were doing on Wednesday night between eleven and two."

"What was I doing?" Harriet took a sharp breath. She appeared confused. "Well, I imagine I was asleep."

"Do you sleep with your husband, Harriet?"

174

There was an instant's hesitation. "With Michael? Well yes, of course."

"And were you sleeping with him on Wednesday night?"

This time the pause was longer. Blusher stood out like two raspberry flags on the pallor of her skin. "Inspector." A brittle protest. "What is this about? I think I have a right to know why I'm being asked such . . . personal questions."

"Of course," Amanda soothed. "Of course you do, Harriet. This is about the murder of an acquaintance of yours, Christopher Clarke."

Harriet repeated the name vaguely. "I'm sorry. I don't recall him . . ."

"An acquaintance of your husband's perhaps?"

"Mikey knows so many people." A simper.

"Was Mr. Wilson with you between the hours I mentioned on Wednesday night, Harriet?"

Harriet's knuckles whitened, her face began to crumble. The Estée Lauder smelled overpowering. Because the woman wearing it was sweating, Amanda guessed.

Harriet finally blurted, "No, he wasn't with me. I . . ." A pause while she fumbled for a fine lawn handkerchief and daintily blew her nose. "This is very humiliating," she whispered. "My husband was not home during those hours. I believe he was at a public . . . bathhouse." Her eyes fluttered to Amanda's, pleading, woman to woman.

Amanda felt a sharp pity. For Harriet and her entire unhappy kind; for the hovering, insecure wives of men like Michael Wilson. "I'm sorry I have to ask you these questions, Harriet," she said more gently. "Please understand they're just routine. We're asking anyone with a connection to the victim."

"Of course." Harriet gripped her engagement ring, twisting it anxiously.

She was pathetic, Amanda decided. Dependent, dried up inside, living a vicarious existence through her husband. What kind of husband was Michael Wilson? A bully. Definitely a bully. How much did Harriet know about his dealings with Clarke? Not a lot, Amanda figured. She probably signed obediently on the dotted line and left the thinking to Mikey.

"When was the last time you saw Chris Clarke?"

"I really don't recall."

"I believe he was your husband's business partner at one stage."

Those carefully penciled lips tightened to a thin red line. "I think it would be best if you spoke to my husband about that." She glanced toward the door. "I don't think I can help you."

Likewise, Amanda thought, staying seated. "Let's talk about your own movements the night of the murder, shall we?" She offered a broad smile. "Where were you at midnight, Harriet?"

"Asleep." Harriet perched forward on her brocade armchair, eyes fixed on the door.

"And where did you say your husband was?"

The insipid hazel eyes flew back to Amanda's, and for a split second they seemed almost calculating. The expression was so fleeting Amanda wondered if it was a trick of the light, or simply a figment of her imagination.

"I said he was at a bathhouse," Harriet responded.

"Which one?"

The other woman produced a contemptuous shrug. "A wife doesn't ask ..."

"What time did you go to bed that night?"

"Ten o'clock. My usual time."

"What time did you last see your husband that day?"

"In the morning," Harriet said coldly. "Michael didn't come home after work."

"I see." Amanda got to her feet. "Thank you for your help, Harriet. I'm sorry if you found this distressing. There's just one more thing." She stared into Harriet's eyes, watching the pupils dilate then contract. "Does your husband own a gun?"

CHAPTER SIXTEEN

Starvation. It could clear the mind, they said. That might be the case for gurus and anyone else who could afford the luxury of contemplating the universe all day. But some of us have to work, Amanda thought, cramming papers into her briefcase.

Austin Shaw had gone off duty, but not before he had obtained the two search warrants Amanda had requested earlier in the day. Fancy footwork, she thought, double-checking that the details were correct.

Shaw had also left an update on "progress" in the Chris Clarke murder inquiry. Based on the tire print and a neighbor's account of seeing a Harley Davidson with a smart-alec plate, Welch had obtained a warrant for Ricky Hippolyte's arrest on suspicion. Hippolyte was thought to have skipped town.

The Clarke autopsy established his time of death at 23:50, Wednesday night. He had suffered fatal chest wounds which were inflicted at a range of four feet. The weapon was a .22 handgun. Regardless of Amanda's theories, Wilson had an alibi for the entire time. Maybe Bob was right. Maybe Ricky did do it.

"Can I get you anything before I go?" Detective Janine Harrison stood before Amanda's desk, bag in hand, about to go off duty.

"No, thanks," Amanda said absently. "Have a nice weekend."

Janine stayed where she was, and, conscious of the younger woman's steady gaze, Amanda looked up.

"Would you like to come out for a bite to eat?" Janine asked.

She was already blushing to the roots of her pretty auburn hair, Amanda noted with a trace of amusement. The poor kid was unbearably transparent; an ambitious young cop who evidently perceived Amanda as mentor and lust object rolled into one.

"That's a kind thought, Janine," Amanda said gently. "Some other time, maybe."

Janine bit her lip. "Inspector. There's something I need to tell you . . ."

Amanda almost winced. Not now, she thought. In

what she hoped was a suitably discouraging tone, she said, "Have a seat."

Janine lowered her bag to the floor and perched on the edge of the chair. "I was on duty on Wednesday night during the Sea of Love raid."

Police business. Amanda whispered a thank you to the Goddess. "Yes," she prompted.

"Something was overlooked in Inspector Welch's report, ma'am."

The ceiling fan droned erratically. Whir. Click. Whir. Click. "Go on," Amanda said.

"The phone call, ma'am. The tip-off. He took that just before twelve midnight."

"The tip-off?"

"Yes, ma'am. About the minors. I put the call through to him. They got my extension by mistake."

"Did you happen to obtain the switchboard trace on the number and address of that call, Janine?"

"Yes." She dived with alacrity into her bag. "Here it is."

Amanda examined the slip of paper. 28 Sorrento Drive. She met Janine's eyes.

"I thought you might want to know," the younger woman said.

Amanda made it home at ten. She'd been so preoccupied she'd forgotten to stop at McDonald's. Strung out, she gazed into her fridge. It contained a large bowl of salad and something chocolatey on a plate. She did a double-take and turned automatically toward the coffee machine. A note was pinned to it. *Last night was great.* Amanda snatched it off and ran nervous fingers through her hair.

A second missive decorated the microwave. *Turn Me On,* it begged. Inside the microwave was what looked like lasagna.

"Oh, no," Amanda groaned out loud. She should never have told Debby where the spare key was.

Her kitchen had been taken over by a Real Woman. If this was what happened after a one-night stand what would a relationship be like? Stress immediately got the better of her and she reached guiltily for the coffee grinder, reminding herself that tomorrow was another day.

While her food was nuking, Amanda listened to her calls.

The deli. *You forgot to phone in your order, Inspector Valentine. Do you want a delivery this weekend? By the way, we all watched your show and we think you're terrific.*

A female voice. Hesitant. Familiar. *Hi. It's Kate here. I just wanted to ring you and tell you I've missed us. Can we have a drink sometime?*

Her father. *Great show, kid. You ever thought about a political career?*

Joe. *Gone fishing for the weekend. See you Monday. How 'bout the California Steak Bar for a change?*

Debby Daley. *Debby here. I'll drop by after work tonight.*

With guilty pleasure, Amanda dragged the lasagna out of the microwave and piled a huge serving onto her plate. Madam was circling her legs intently. Amanda benevolently shoveled some lasagna into a cat bowl for her. If it was good enough for Garfield ...

Devouring her food, she ruminated over the evidence until her brain felt like mush. Eventually she reached the only conclusion she could.

She rang Joe. "You know that theory I said I had."

Silence.

"Look, I know you're fishing, Joe. But I can't ask anyone else."

More silence.

"It's Hippolyte. There's a warrant out for his arrest. We've got to get to him before Bob does."

"Why?"

"Because if my theory's correct he can blow Wilson's alibi clean apart."

"Supposing I said yes. Where do I find the little creep?"

"I don't know, but I think Jezebel does. After all —" Amanda wished she could see Joe's face. "Ricky's her son."

"What?"

"I was surprised too."

When he spoke again it was with awe. "Then Jezebel ..."

"Used to do it with girls?"

"Once, at least." He sounded sheepish. "Why ... if ..." He fell silent, cleared his throat.

"If Jezebel's a *bona fide* father then how come he wears a dress now and does it with boys?"

"Jesus wept, Amanda!" Clearly Joe's men's group hadn't dealt with transsexuality yet.

Amanda smirked. "I hear where you're coming from, Joe."

"Yeah, Disneyland."

"You'll do it then?"

"What makes you think Jezebel will tell us where he is ... I mean she's trying to protect him, right?"

"I think she'll tell you, Joe."

"Why?" He sounded blank.

"She thinks you're cute. She told me so."

"Jesus."

Amanda could hear him hyperventilating. "She's at Roseanne's beach cottage in Otaki."

"Otaki." Joe sounded mollified. "Now we're talking."

Amanda smiled. "I hear the trout are biting up there, too."

Amanda stowed her empty plate in the dishwasher and lovingly transported the chocolate thing into the sitting room. She devoured it along with a double espresso. The texture was wonderful, thick, silken; the flavor unbearably intense. She wanted more before she had even finished the first bite. It was incredible, the culinary equivalent of a delayed orgasm.

After the final soul-shattering mouthful, she glanced at her watch, lay back with her eyes closed and hated herself for listening for a yuppie car. She visualized making love with Debby, holding her afterward, damp and content. Her mind wandered in an unfenced field consisting of alarming images like

Debby living in her house, Debby in her bed every night.

Irritated at her train of thought, she got up and stalked to her bedroom. It was immaculate, oddly symmetrical. Fresh sheets were on the bed and a clean cotton nightshirt lay folded on her pillow. Gone was the wild tangle of clothes on the floor, the astounding mixture of scents she'd left behind that morning.

It was the same in the bathroom. Everything smelled of cleaning fluid. Even the showerbox. But something was different, the mood of the room had somehow mellowed. Puzzled, Amanda stared around the walls. The lightbulbs. They had been swapped for lower wattage.

It unnerved her totally. In all the time she and Kate were lovers this had never happened. Kate had never touched anything, changed anything. She had never intruded on Amanda's life in any way.

Shaken, Amanda returned to the sitting room to find Debby on the sofa calmly reading a magazine. She looked up, eyes dark with promise, and, halfway between rage and desire, Amanda walked over and removed the magazine from her hands.

Without a word, she pulled Debby to her feet and immediately slid a hand up her dress, past her perfect thighs into the damp space between them. Really sophisticated. Stifling Debby's small startled gasp with her mouth, Amanda kissed her hard and passionately. Then she carried her into the bedroom, dumped her unceremoniously on the bed and rolled on top of her.

As she dragged Debby's dress off, stared

worshipfully at her immaculate form and buried her face in those astounding breasts, Amanda knew she was in trouble.

She woke the next morning feeling ashamed. Debby was already up and making coffee in the kitchen. She acknowledged Amanda with a brief smile but her eyes were clouded with reproach.

Amanda slunk into the bathroom and stood under the shower. How low could you sink, she wondered. Imagine making love with a woman and pretending she was someone else. It hadn't been conscious. At first she didn't even realize the voice repeating Kelly's name was her own. But as Debby's body tensed and withdrew, Amanda realized what she had done.

"Who is Kelly?" Debby had whispered, crushing the sheet across her breasts with white knuckles.

Amanda was silent, shaken. Tears filled her eyes. She couldn't say it. She felt sick, humiliated. It was five years, for God's sake. She'd had dozens of lovers over that time and nothing like this had ever happened.

"I'm sorry," she'd murmured finally and rolled away from Debby to stare at the wall.

She had lain there, tears trickling steadily into her pillow. After a while she'd felt Debby's hand leave her shoulder and heard her crying softly. Eventually her breathing had taken on the even rhythm of sleep and Amanda had slipped out of bed to make herself a coffee.

In the darkness she'd sat in front of the dead TV screen and thought about Kelly. Kelly with the black shiny curls and the bold eyes; the woman who'd been attacked while she was jogging and had rewarded her assailant with a broken jaw and a shattered kneecap.

Amanda had been fresh out of the Police Academy when she was assigned to take down a statement from the black-belt jogger. She'd been so bowled over she could hardly stammer out her routine questions. When Kelly had phoned her a few days later for a date, she had been mortified. How had Kelly known? Amanda was so far into the closet back then she even wore what passed for an engagement ring and dragged a football jock cousin along to parties.

At first she told herself Kelly was just asking her out because she'd been decent about the attack. Plenty of cops might have asked Kelly what she was wearing and wisecracked when she said shorts.

After several dates Kelly had asked frankly, "There's no fiance, is there, Amanda?"

Amanda shook her head and guiltily twisted her pseudo-engagement ring. "I wear it so the guys will leave me alone."

"You want guys to leave you alone?"

Amanda bit her lip.

"I'm a lesbian too," Kelly told her. "Only I'm out."

Amanda stammered. "How did you know . . ."

"It was your eyes," Kelly said blandly. "When you interviewed me you didn't know where to look, did you?"

Amanda remembered Kelly in her hospital bed, sitting on the covers in short pajamas. She had great legs, followed closely by her wonderful rounded stomach and full breasts, her knockout smile and her thick, fabulous black hair.

Amanda had stared like the village idiot. "I'm, er . . ." she'd begun and promptly forgot her own name.

Kelly had laughed. "I thought I was the one who got hit over the head."

They had kept up a farce of dating for several months, then moved in together. Life wasn't perfect. Amanda was a cop and firmly in the closet; Kelly was a scientist who wore lambda earrings. But they were in love, madly, extravagantly in love.

They fought sometimes, especially over Amanda's job. It was after one of those fights that Kelly had driven in to the precinct to make amends.

The gunman had arrived seconds before her, looking for the cop who'd killed his brother. The desk sergeant had sounded the alarm before the guy pulled his piece. Every cop in the place was converging on him.

Kelly had chosen that moment to walk in and gasp loudly. The punk had turned and emptied his chambers into her, extinguishing the heartbeat that had lulled Amanda to sleep for four years.

Even now she could close her eyes and hear that heartbeat thumping quietly in the recesses of her mind.

Holding her face to the blast of the shower, her throat closing first on one sob then another, Amanda leaned against the tiled wall, shoulders heaving.

Five years. Five years and the pain was still unbearable.

* * * * *

Amanda took her time getting dressed. She knew Debby was waiting for her. She could imagine the conversation. *Well, I'll be seeing you. It was nice while it lasted.* A civilized kiss. No hard feelings.

She stole downstairs, preparing herself to be adult. Debby was sitting at the dining table reading a newspaper. She was wigless and wearing glasses.

Amanda stood in the doorway and felt stupid. Debby's wide-eyed stare suddenly made sense. The woman was short-sighted.

"Oh, hi!" Debby saw her and, coloring slightly, whipped off the glasses. "I'll make you some breakfast." She moved into the kitchen and started bustling around.

"No!" Amanda said and immediately regretted the harshness of her tone. "I mean, I'd rather you didn't."

Debby's eyes flicked warily across her face. "Is it over between us? Just say so if it is."

Amanda hesitated, muddled at the direction of the conversation. It was up to her, it seemed. She could say goodbye now, before things got complicated and people got hurt. She thought about Debby's warm smooth body. She thought about waking alone every morning, about seeing Debby on television every now and then.

"No," she said hoarsely. "It's not over."

"You don't sound very happy about that." Debby regarded her steadily.

Amanda yanked at her hair and scowled. "I'm just stressed."

"Over something at work?"

That too, Amanda thought. At the rate things were going she'd probably arrive at the Station after her weekend off duty, to find herself off the Big Mack Task Force and placed in charge of the Annual Charity Ball.

"You want to tell me about it?"

Debby headed for the sitting room. Amanda wandered after her, enjoying the curve of her buttocks beneath the silky bathrobe.

"It's a long story," she warned, collapsing on the sofa.

Undeterred, her paramour settled in an armchair, tucked her feet beneath her and delicately wet her lips. "If you've got the notion, honey, I've got the time."

The net was closing, Amanda persuaded herself late in the morning. She wallowed in self-praise for several seconds. What magnificent planning, what exquisite timing. Yes, a detective lived for such moments. Only hours from now, she would solve two murders and reveal corrupt practices that would embarrass bigshots all over town. Maybe she would also get a decent night's sleep.

Joe had called from Otaki to advise that he knew where to find Ricky Hippolyte and he would be driving to Napier the next day to pick him up. Meantime Jezebel was packing a picnic and they were on their way up the Otaki River to fish.

From Austin Shaw, Amanda learned that she still had a job and that the Paekakariki doorknock had turned up several residents who claimed to have seen Donnelly's car driving along Ocean View Road sometime in December. There were two men in the car, they claimed. Descriptions varied. No one had seen anyone resembling "Mary."

Shaw doubted whether it would be diplomatic to question the Deputy Mayor. They had nothing concrete. He wasn't even sure Amanda should talk to Wilson on Monday. They stood to lose a lot of credibility.

Preoccupied, Amanda turned up at her Saturday afternoon hairdresser's appointment. Debby had arranged it.

The place looked like a gallery. Weird cloth sculptures reclined along the walls and everything was black and white, including the staff. A woman with dark eyes and a crew cut surveyed Amanda's sensible style with an expression of stoned horror. "Look, Roger," she told a man with a white feather swinging from one ear. "It's almost a pageboy."

"I cut it myself in between times," Amanda explained.

The woman shuddered. "Next time practice on your wrists."

A couple of hours later, Amanda's hair had a very short back and sides and a dense cowlick. They'd bleached her ash blonde hair a shade or two lighter and groaned when Amanda said it made her dark eyebrows look fake. People paid money for that, they said.

The hairdresser asked Amanda if she was in theater.

"I'm a cop."

"A woman in uniform. How thrilling."

"I don't get to wear the uniform very often."

Dark eyes flashed in the mirror at her. "Pity." The woman slipped something into Amanda's hand. A small white card. "That's me," she explained. "If you want a haircut, give me a ring. If you want anything else, give me a ring too."

After the hairdresser, Amanda got brave and went shopping. She never usually bothered. Clothes didn't interest her a whole lot. As she trudged listlessly from boutique to boutique, she could see why. The whole business was mindless and boring. She wouldn't be doing it if it weren't for Debby Daley, she realized with blinding candor.

After a particularly harrowing experience in one of those claustrophobic mirrored changing rooms, she abandoned the entire depressing business for more comforting territory: food. Mistaking discontent for hunger, she invested in a double chocolate ice cream, and plunked herself down on a bench in the mall.

Everyone around her was just going about their business, innocent of the daily horrors that preoccupied her as a cop. They looked around and saw color, shop fronts, a bustling crowd. Amanda's view involved sizing up alarm systems, matching faces in the crowd with mental wanted posters, remembering murders committed in this vicinity. She heaved a sigh. You were never a cop only eight hours a day.

Then there was Kate. Amanda hadn't returned her phone call. She'd been too busy. Did she want to see Kate anyway? Guilt gnawed at her like a weary rat. Kate was a woman she respected and cared about. Why was she treating her like a leper? She thought about the way their relationship had ended and felt queasy.

Kate had been hurt. It was a wonder she was prepared to see Amanda at all, let alone initiate it. What did she want? Amanda pictured an attempt to rekindle the relationship and felt ashamed of her egocentricity. Maybe Kate just planned to slap her face or something. God knows she deserved it.

She watched a pair of woman wander past, hands loosely joined, and felt a peculiar grief wash over her. She saw herself walking with Kelly on holiday in San Francisco, young, carefree, optimistic.

She'd almost forgotten that lightness, that inviolate contentment. She wondered if she would ever feel it again.

After a couple of more hours of desultory browsing and wondering what she was doing goofing off when there was crime to be solved, Amanda checked the time and headed along Manners Mall.

Although she was officially off-duty, she was still preoccupied with the two homicide inquiries dominating her life. *It's time,* her inner voice informed her. Amanda rejected the notion. It couldn't be time. The pieces were there but they still didn't quite fit. Every time she caught a glimpse of the whole picture, some part of it slid out of reach, a casualty of her literal mind.

It was too soon to spring the trap she had dreamed up. She had not yet assembled all the evidence. And worst of all, she was acting autonomously, outside of accepted procedure. There was no choice, she reflected bitterly. She couldn't afford to expose herself when she had no idea how high the chain of corruption went. She wished she could talk with the Chief, but that wasn't a risk she was prepared to take. She knew that if he were in her shoes he would do the same.

It's Saturday night, she told herself. Loosen up a little. Have some fun. Vacillating, she stuffed her hands into her pockets, only to withdraw one immediately, the fingers closed around a scrap of paper. For a split second she stared at it, then she headed for a phone booth, hoping Jezebel was back from her fishing expedition.

After making the call, she contemplated dropping by the Station, but her stomach was making small whining noises. Besides, Roseanne would never forgive her if she canceled another of their dinner dates.

Hastening her pace, she tried to ignore the kids sniffing glue and the deros being kicked off the park benches the punks wanted to use. She usually avoided this route. It always made her late and caught her flak from Uniform Branch for poaching on their beat.

She could see Roseanne, a slight figure clinging to the balustrade by the old Bank of New Zealand building. Spotting Amanda, she waved and began squeezing her way through a mob of street kids, exchanging brief words with the ones she knew.

Roseanne was Amanda's closest friend. She was also a social worker. The kind who always got involved in her cases, sometimes had them living with her, and couldn't walk up the street without some waif nailing her for a bus fare. They called her Mom. When Amanda had questioned that she was quickly put in her place. It's the only chance some of them have to use the word, Roseanne had told her piously.

As usual, Roseanne's Fiat hatchback was packed with minors destined for the Railway Station. Holding her breath, Amanda squeezed into the front seat and wound down her window. Behind her, a plastic bag rustled and she turned around in time to see a girl lift it to her face.

"Give me that!" She tore it away from the kid.

"Hey, man!" the girl wailed.

"Christ, Amanda!" Roseanne grabbed her arm. "What the hell's wrong with you? Give it back to her."

"I'm not sitting here while you let juveniles kill themselves sniffing solvents," Amanda said, waving the bag under Roseanne's nose. Inside was a bread roll.

"Shit." Amanda stared down at the mangled remains and picked a piece of beetroot off her jeans. "Pull over will you, Roseanne? By that burger joint." She glanced over her shoulder at Roseanne's sullen passengers and muttered, "Looks like I'm buying."

"You seem pretty stressed," Roseanne observed half an hour later over a large bowl of fettuccine.

"Is it that obvious?"

"Only if you notice the black rings and the short fuse."

Amanda groaned.

"It's a woman," Roseanne guessed. She could read Amanda like a book and besides, as she often

194

reminded Amanda, she dealt with cot cases for a living. "Is it love?"

"Of course not. We're sleeping together, that's all."

"So what's eating you then?" A giggle. "Sorry, couldn't resist it."

"Very funny," Amanda grunted. "Well ... I think about her all the time. I can't seem to stop myself. It's turning into some kind of sick obsession."

"Infatuation," Roseanne said happily. "How romantic."

"Don't be ridiculous. Christ, you know me, Roseanne. I'm just not a romantic. If I'm going to bed with someone, I'm going to bed with them. Easy come, easy go."

"Like Kate?"

Amanda grimaced. "You could make a good living hiring yourself out to salt wounds, lady."

"She was very upset. It wasn't easy come, easy go for her."

"I never wanted that," Amanda said defensively. "I never asked her to get involved."

"Why not?"

"You know why not!" She downed her cheap red wine and banged the glass down on the table. The waitress gave her a filthy look.

Roseanne smirked. "My, we are tense. So you're still hanging onto that strong, silent crap. Kelly's dead and buried. Do you think she'd want you to spend the rest of your life punishing yourself over what happened? You can't keep measuring every woman you meet against her, Amanda. No one can compete with a memory."

"I'm not looking for a replacement."

"I know that." Roseanne took her hand across the table. "You can't replace someone you love who dies. But you can stop blaming yourself for what happened."

"If Kelly hadn't been my lover she would still be alive," Amanda blurted. "If I wasn't a cop she would never have been in the precinct that day. If we weren't lovers she wouldn't have come all the way into town to kiss and make up."

"So what's the answer? Become a hermit, or a workaholic maybe? Everyone who ever lost someone can find a thousand ways to blame themselves. Let it go, Amanda! Or you'll be the second victim of that gunman forever."

Amanda poured another glass of wine and sipped it distractedly. "Don't you think I've tried? I thought I was doing okay. Then I met her."

"Do I know her?"

"You could say that. She's very, er . . . unusual."

"So cut the suspense."

"She's in the media. Her name's Debby Daley."

The smile froze on Roseanne's face. "Debby Daley. *The* Debby Daley."

"The very same," Amanda said dryly.

Roseanne threw her a penetrating look. Amanda could tell what she was thinking. It was a nice safe way for her to avoid issues. Fall for a straight woman. Or an airhead.

"I had no idea she was a dyke," said Roseanne cautiously.

"Neither did I."

"But you're in a relationship with her?"

"We've gone to bed a couple of times, hardly a marriage."

"Sounds like your style then." A touch of acid. "So what's the problem?"

"Jesus, Roseanne. Do I have to spell it out? I've fallen for her like a ton of bricks. I haven't felt this way since Marcia Schwarzkopf in the eighth grade for Godsake."

"So congratulations. Welcome to the real world. People do get crushes, you know."

"I have to stop it before it's too late."

Roseanne burst out laughing. "Too late! Too late for what?"

"Well I'm glad you're amused. I happen to be serious about this. I don't have time for emotional complications in my life."

"What about Debby? Maybe there's less of a problem than you think. Maybe she doesn't want to get serious either."

"That's what's so bizarre. She says she's not interested in getting involved but she makes dinner for me and does the washing. I can't stand it."

"Maybe that's just her cute way of thanking you for showing her a good time."

Amanda snorted. "Most people do it with flowers."

"Debby Daley doesn't look like most people to me."

"I'll tell her it's off," Amanda said.

"Chicken," Roseanne flapped her arms, to the horror of the waiting staff.

"I've got no choice."

Roseanne looked annoyed. "Then don't waste my time wimping about it. Amanda, you're my dearest friend and I love you but honestly, sometimes ..."

"Give me a break, Rosy."

"No, give yourself a break. Fall in love for a change. It might give you a whole new perspective on life." Roseanne waved for the dessert menu. Therapy time was over.

Debby's BMW was parked outside Amanda's place with its lights off. Debby looked like she'd been there a while. Amanda beat back the urge to lift her bodily from the car and carry her inside like Tarzan. Instead she tapped politely on the window and watched Debby's eyelids lift slowly. The door opened.

"What are you doing here?" Amanda asked.

Debby dragged herself wearily from her seat. "I've had a tough day."

Amanda slipped an arm around her waist, enjoying the way Debby's head drooped against her shoulder as they walked indoors. "It's late. You should be at home in bed."

"I had to see you."

"What's the rush?"

"I'm going to Auckland tomorrow for a couple of interviews."

Amanda immediately felt her stomach churn. "Auckland," she repeated with a hollow ring. She found herself gazing at Debby's feet. They'd slipped out of her shoes and the toes were kneading the carpet. She was looking stunning in a purple off-the-shoulder top and a black lycra mini-skirt. She wore ultrasheer black stockings with seams up the back. Amanda imagined those legs curling around her and was immediately disgusted at herself. Sex junkie.

Debby was sighing. "He's a real jerk. I would never normally have him on the show but he's a bosom buddy of Max Jacobs, that's the programming manager and well . . ."

Amanda lifted her gaze from Debby's crotch and tried to get her act together. "So what? I mean, it's your show."

"That's just the point." Debby's huge eyes were suddenly overflowing. "If I want to keep it that way I have to go along with Max."

"Why?"

"It's a long story." She sounded defeated. "They're on my back to take on a co-presenter, a guy."

"What the hell for?"

Debby laughed harshly. "I'm too popular. They're scared shitless that I'm going to hit them up for bigger bikkies or sell out to another station. They want to bring in one of the boys and get him established so they've got something to fall back on. Only they're calling it giving the show some balance. The *Wheel of Fortune* formula. The hunk talks, the bimbo walks."

"They can't be that stupid."

"This is showbiz, Amanda. If they can drop a yes boy into my show and keep the ratings exactly where they are, they'll be laughing all the way to the bank."

"You can't let that happen."

"What do you suggest?"

"Ever thought of setting up a production company?"

Debby shook her head. "You're talking money. I don't have that much."

"Other people do. You could find investors. I'm sure of it."

"I love your confidence, but meantime I'm stuck with interviewing that creep Rollo."

"Rollo?" The name was vaguely familiar.

"Douglas Rollo. He owns a whole lot of clubs around Auckland. I've met him a couple of times and he's a total sleaze. Thinks he's God's gift."

Amanda stretched a sympathetic arm across her shoulders. "I wish I could come with you," she said, startling even herself.

Debby lifted her eyes. The dullness was gone and they shone with surprise and happiness. "Do you mean it? You'd really come with me?"

"If I could."

"But you're working on the Chris Clarke murder, right?"

Amanda hesitated. "Not officially."

Debby's eyes were laser bright. "What do you mean?"

"I mean I'm working on it but another detective has actually been assigned to the case. At the moment I'm not reporting to him."

Debby looked puzzled, then her features flooded with comprehension and she planted an excited kiss squarely on Amanda's mouth. "That's the nicest thing anyone has ever done for me!"

Amanda smiled weakly.

Debby's eyes were radiant. "I can't wait to see Max's face when I pull off that story." She kissed Amanda again. "As soon as you work out who killed him, I'll put the whole feature together."

It sounded so simple. "What do you mean, put it together?" Amanda asked uneasily.

"The show. Chris Clarke. The drug racket. The killings. I've worked it all out. You should see what I've got on him." She smiled with deep satisfaction.

Amanda felt lightheaded. Diminished brainmass, she decided. It was the only explanation. How else could she, Amanda Valentine, detective extraordinaire, have been so patently outdistanced by a media bimbo?

"I'd really like to see what you've got on him," she told Debby.

"You mean now?"

"Yes, please."

Debby leapt up and said she'd just get something from her car. Moments later she returned, dumped a stack of papers in front of Amanda, and inserted a video cassette in the player.

She wound the tape past some scenic shots, explaining, "This is the East Cape and the Coromandel ... you know, where all the dope plantations are. Chris Clarke thought he was so smart," she said disgustedly. "He bought all these farms off bankrupt farmers then leased them back for peanuts. In return the farmers had to grow a crop for him."

"How do you know that?" Amanda demanded.

"Watch," said Debby.

Startled, Amanda listened to two men interviewed

in silhouette. Both described the very process Debby had just explained. Both claimed they were too frightened to back out.

"There's lots of that kind of stuff on the tape," Debby said in a matter-of-fact tone. "Of course he's in hard drugs as well — everything, really. I talked to this woman ..." She wound the tape on. "Here she is."

A shrouded figure described operating as a courier for Clarke. She was picked up in King's Cross, Sydney, supporting a habit and a two-year-old child. Clarke had offered her some easy money to transport heroin out of Bangkok. She did it for a year, then Clarke decided she'd had too much exposure. He kept her on to recruit new couriers for him.

"She wanted to get out," Debby said. "But she knew too much. She said there's only one way you leave that business."

"So how come she talked to you?"

"I told her you were on to Clarke and she could plea bargain if she was prepared to be a prosecution witness. I said you'd protect her."

"Jesus, Debby! This isn't *L.A. Law.*"

Her lover gazed at her innocently. "Well you would, wouldn't you?"

With an expressive groan, Amanda returned her attention to the video. Debby had really done her homework. She had assembled a complex picture of Clarke's lifestyle, his ruthlessness and his status in the drug world. Most of it was hearsay, but there was still enough to open an investigation.

"Shame he's dead," Amanda remarked.

"Those who live by the sword ..." Debby looked wry. "What amazes me is how he got away with it. He must have been paying someone to shut up."

"Possibly," Amanda said in a noncommittal tone.

Debby's eyes narrowed. "I was kind of hoping you might be able to tell me who it was."

"Is that why you're dating me?"

"Oh, sure." Debby laughed, moving into Amanda's arms and pressing a suggestive knee between her thighs.

Amanda found herself staring straight into the dark valley between Debby's breasts. "I mean it," she murmured thickly. "Why?"

Debby was kissing her hair, her forehead, her eyelids. "For the sex, of course." She met Amanda's eyes with a provocative smile and started unbuttoning her shirt.

Amanda slid her hands beneath Debby's tight little skirt to curve around her buttocks. "You know, you shouldn't wear this in public," she muttered. It was supposed to be a gentle tease but somehow the tone was all wrong.

Debby looked back at her sharply and her cheeks went pink. "You're jealous," she accused.

"Of course I'm not!" Amanda jerked out a swift denial.

"It's written all over your face. You're imagining other women looking at me, aren't you?"

Amanda caught Debby's shoulders and bent to kiss her throat. The skin was warm and smooth and smelt faintly of amaryllis. She nibbled where the shoulders hollowed and began tugging at the buttons holding Debby's top together. "I'm not jealous," she murmured again.

"I don't believe you," Debby said breathlessly.

Amanda pulled the shirt off and threw it over the side of the sofa. Underneath Debby was wearing a white lace bra. Amanda couldn't work out what would turn her on more — leaving it there or getting rid of it. She trailed her fingertips across it and felt Debby's nipples tighten beneath the fine layers, then she lowered her head and bit where her fingertips had been.

"I once had a lover who used to *tear* my clothes off," Debby announced placidly.

Amanda stopped what she was doing and pulled a ragged breath. "I don't want to hear about some other lover of yours."

Debby's eyes were wide and innocent. "Well, I'm sorry. I thought you said you weren't jealous."

"Goddamn it, I'm not!" Amanda yanked the bra off and hurled it at the television. "I just don't need to hear a catalogue of your former lovers' accomplishments right now."

"I've never done it on a sofa," Debby offered gravely. Her hands were pulling Amanda's shirt out of her pants.

Amanda shivered as the hands made contact with her bare flesh. "Keep on talking and you never will either."

Debby kissed her intently. "She used to carry me to the bedroom too," she said against Amanda's mouth, then squealed as she was lifted bodily off the sofa.

"So she was really butch, huh?" Amanda

muttered as she carried Debby toward her room. "Big deal."

"Not jealous are you?"

"Should I be?" She lowered Debby to the bed and rolled the scandalous mini out of the way. "I mean, do you still sleep with her?"

"What if I do?" Debby parted her thighs and squirmed as Amanda blew warm air between them.

Amanda rested her head on Debby's stomach for a moment and registered the question. She could smell Debby, her perfume, her wetness, the slight saltiness of her skin. She couldn't stand the idea that any other woman might recognize those smells too. "Are you seeing someone else?" she demanded.

Debby's eyes met hers, wild ocean blue, dark with passion. She traced her lips with her tongue. "Does it matter?"

Amanda's nerve ends leapt, her heart crashed against her chest. "Yes, it matters," she finally jerked out.

"Good," said Debby and pulled her down into a hard embrace. "Prove it."

Several hours later Amanda lay drifting in that phantom half-world between consciousness and sleep, a multitude of impressions kaleidescoped in her head; bright fragments shifting repeatedly, each time creating a new and singular pattern. When finally they halted, Amanda was confronted with a design of such dazzling symmetry, such intricate detail, that her body froze with shock.

Shivering, she opened her eyes and elbowed herself upright. *I know who you are,* she whispered.

Then the phone rang.

"It's me. Jezebel."

Amanda glanced at Debby. She hadn't woken. "What's doing?"

"He's hot to trot, lovie."

"Good. You set up the meeting?"

"Six in the morning, just like you said. Don't know when a girl's expected to sleep."

Amanda smiled. "What did you tell him?"

"Just exactly what you said, lovie. Twenty grand up front and he gets the book."

"Okay. I'll pick you up at five-thirty and we'll go down to the motel."

"You're picking me up?"

"Is that a problem?"

There was a split second's hesitation.

"Jezebel ..."

"You never said nothing 'bout picking me up, doll. That walk would of ruined my heels. I just didn't see no point."

Amanda took a deep breath. "You gave him your address?"

Silence. Then, "Oh, sweet Jesus."

"Jezebel." Amanda injected her voice with calm. "When did you make that call?"

" 'Bout twenty minutes ago ... We got trouble?"

Amanda visualized Jezebel alone and carless in

Roseanne's tiny secluded beach cottage an hour out of Wellington. "Yes," she groaned. "We've got a shitload."

CHAPTER SEVENTEEN

"Where are you going?" Debby murmured.

"Just a routine callout." Amanda pulled the Smith & Wesson from her bedside drawer. Maybe it was time she retired the trusty K frame .357 Magnum in favor of the latest technology, she reflected. Stroking the mother-of-pearl grips, she tried to imagine herself packing a grunt weapon, say a .45 ACP, maybe that new 14-shot automatic, silent reloading . . . all the trimmings.

The prospect failed to move her. The fact was she had formed a grotesque sentimental attachment to a handgun. The S & W had saved her ass more than once and she'd never had to kill anyone with it yet, not counting pit bulls. Bearing that in mind, she felt a whole lot better loading in the six heavy little slugs that could do the job if necessary.

"That must weigh a ton." Debby watched her belt her holster and slide the .357 home. "I thought New Zealand police were meant to be unarmed."

"In general they are. Although these days we keep a handgun in virtually every patrol car."

"But you wear yours."

"It wouldn't do me a whole lot of good in the glovebox," Amanda said dryly.

"What's the callout?" Debby was sitting up, alert suddenly. "You're not going out to the garbage dump, are you?"

"No."

"I could come with you."

"It's two in the morning. Go back to sleep."

Debby climbed out of bed and padded across the carpet, nestling against Amanda's back. "I could wait in the car."

Amanda turned. "Don't ask," she said softly. "I find it hard to say no to you."

Debby pressed her mouth to Amanda's. "Then say yes."

For a moment Amanda allowed herself to be seduced by the idea, to imagine Debby traveling the mean streets with her; a sister voyager in the hostile landscape that was policework. Moonlight illuminated Debby's face, the lace of the curtains dappling her skin with gauzy shadows. She looked so innocent and lovely, so trusting. So unknowing.

Oddly moved, Amanda touched her cheek. "I'll come home soon," she said. "I promise."

Amanda headed for the station, phone in one hand, steering wheel in the other.

The Sergeant had a few problems with Roseanne's address and getting two cars out there to the sticks within forty minutes was definitely going to present difficulties. It was Saturday night and a gang brawl was underway in Wainuiomata, all available units in attendance.

He put Amanda through to CI9 with the promise that he'd do his best. Maybe Paraparaumu, a bit further up the coast, could help. Janine Harrison took the CI9 call.

"I didn't know you were on the graveyard shift," Amanda commented.

"I swapped with Joe." A hesitation as Janine evidently recalled the rules about swapping within your rank. "The DSS cleared it."

Thank God for the bureaucracy. "I'm on my way in. Get a car and meet me out front."

"Now?" Janine gasped audibly.

"Yes, now. You got a piece?"

"A what?"

Jesus. "A gun, Harrison."

"Yes, ma'am."

"Load it for Chrissakes. I'll see you in five minutes."

* * * * *

Roseanne's cottage was a rustic, two-bedroomed affair with verandas all around and fragrant hedgerow gardens. The place was an hour or so out of Wellington in a small coastal settlement called Otaki. It was the kind of spot people retired to. Quiet, sunny, golden beaches, lots of churches. In January it was packed with nuclear families who'd fled the city for their summer vacations.

Janine mopped her face as the car jerked to a halt, wheels spinning in the gravel of Roseanne's narrow driveway. "Looks like we beat them," she gasped.

"Put your head down for a minute," Amanda said, taking in the young woman's pallor. They'd managed the trip in forty-five minutes, floorboarding all the way. No wonder the kid was carsick.

Flicking the headlights down, Amanda negotiated her way behind the cottage, parking under cover of the dense bush. "Let's go," she told Harrison. "I'll take the back."

Before she could reach the door, it swung open and Jezebel greeted her with an ecstatic sigh. Calling Harrison, Amanda locked the door behind them and quickly cased the cottage. It was your typical cheap bach, rooms added hodge podge when the owner could afford it. From the kitchen, a short corridor led to the front door. Off this was a sitting room which opened to a single bedroom.

Amanda stationed Harrison in the bedroom with instructions to use her own initiative. Hopefully, Wilson would be stupid enough to come alone. But Amanda doubted it.

Just before three, a car crawled slowly up the

drive. Two men emerged. Both were large, meaty-fisted specimens wearing cheap suits. The smaller had a slight limp; Sucker Dawson. Another piece of the picture fell neatly into place. Michael Wilson was nowhere in sight.

Jezebel was anxiously pacing the corridor.

"Just do exactly what I told you," Amanda whispered and took her place behind the kitchen door.

There was a loud knock.

Jezebel counted to five then yelled, "Who is that?"

The handle twisted back and forth and Amanda could make out some mumbling.

"Mr. Wilson sent us," a voice shouted. "Open up."

"Quit that racket," Jezebel bellowed. "You'll disturb the neighbors."

"Open up, lady, or we'll hafta do it for ya."

Jezebel toyed with the lock. "Who did you say sent you?"

"Mr. Wilson. The Mayor, okay?"

Jezebel unfastened the lock and opened the door. "Well, why didn't you say so in the first place," she said. "Mr. Wilson didn't tell me nothing about two big handsome boys like you coming on ahead."

"You got somefink for Mister Wilson?" Sucker Dawson demanded. It was probably the longest speech he'd ever made, Amanda thought.

"I certainly have," Jezebel replied. "Wait in there." She indicated the small sitting room. Sucker Dawson stuck his head in the door while his companion stayed where he was, in the passageway.

This guy was a real gorilla; dark designer stubble, Schwarzenegger haircut. Looked like he belonged on a chain. "So get the parcel," he ordered Jezebel.

She stood where she was. "You got the money?"

"Get the parcel first."

Jezebel was staring at them intently. "Don't I know you boys from somewhere?"

"Maybe." The gorilla moved toward her with a menacing expression.

Jezebel flung her hand across her mouth. "You're the ones," she announced shrilly. "You're the lowlife . . ."

"She remembers," Sucker Dawson began.

"Shuddup," the gorilla snarled.

Jezebel raised an arm and pointed theatrically. "You're the scum that trashed my flat and half-killed me with that crowbar!"

The gorilla folded his arms and gave Dawson a nod.

Dawson reached inside his jacket and produced a short iron bar.

Jezebel wrung her hands and burst into loud sobs. "Scum of the earth."

Sucker Dawson caught hold of her, twisting her arms behind her back.

"Say, mate," the gorilla crooned at Dawson, "I never seen a broad as ugly as this." He twisted a fold of Jezebel's cheek between two fingers.

Dawson sniggered. "That ain't a broad. That's one of them, you know, transvestals."

The gorilla nodded. "Ya don't say." He flashed a

sinister grin at Jezebel, then brought up a swift knee into her groin. "So where is it, ya pervert?" he demanded.

Jezebel was sobbing. "It's in the kitchen. Cupboard above the stove."

"I'll get it," the gorilla told Sucker Dawson. "You take care of the queen."

Sucker nodded. "Ya mean . . ."

"No," Jezebel wailed. "Please don't kill me. I won't say nothin' bout all of this."

The gorilla was making his way to the kitchen. "I'll tell ya when," he called across his shoulder.

Dawson grunted and dragged Jezebel into the sitting room. Amanda could hear her yelling insults. Then there was an abrupt silence. Amanda hoped Janine Harrison was the cause of it.

The gorilla walked carelessly through the kitchen door, staring straight up at the cupboard. There was a chair conveniently beside the stove. He heaved it into position and climbed up, stretching his arms above his shoulders to force the rusted old lock.

As he was reaching inside the cupboard, Amanda emerged from behind the door and stealthily crossed the tiny room. Sliding the barrel of her .357 between his legs, she said, "One false move and you're a choirboy, sonny. Now drop those arms one at a time, real slow."

The gorilla turned slightly to peer down at her. Amanda jabbed the gun harder and he winced and lowered his arms.

Reaching for her cuffs, she kicked the chair out from under him. But he must have sensed her intent. As the chair fell, he leapt straight at her, scissoring her between powerful thighs and hurling her violently toward the stove. Amanda instinctively stretched out her arms to save herself and the .357 flew from her fingers.

In an instant the gorilla had kick-boxed her hard behind the kneecaps, and she was down on the floor. The gun was out of reach, lying a few feet away under the table. He saw it too and threw himself onto Amanda to stop her moving.

He fought like a street fighter, but Amanda's hands were free and she went first for his eyes, then his kidneys. For a big guy, he was slippery. He moved fast and unexpectedly. Just as she was pinning his shoulders, he managed to slide a knee up and throw her off.

She crashed heavily into the door and scrambled up as he was making a dive for the gun. He got a grip on it and took a single wayward shot as Amanda hit the deck and rolled.

Back on her feet, she caught him off balance as he was trying to turn the gun on her. A second shot went wide as she kicked him in the spine. Smashing his arms with all her force against the heavy table leg, she made him drop the gun.

"Need any help, Inspector?" an earnest voice inquired from the doorway, and Janine Harrison picked up the Smith & Wesson, dusted it off, and politely handed it to her.

CHAPTER EIGHTEEN

The sky was soggy grey when Amanda arrived at the Station. Austin Shaw, that paragon of exactitude, had already prepared the charges against Dawson and his buddy. He had them in separate interview rooms sweating in their own juices. Neither of them possessed feet worthy of comparison with the alleged footprint of the Garbage Dump Killer, he sorrowfully informed Amanda.

"Is Bob on duty this weekend?" she asked.

Shaw shook his head. "Don't think so. I heard he's out of town."

With the issue of search warrants, and with Donnelly's sketch of Wilson pinned to the wall, an air of controlled excitement had pervaded the Task Force. Could the Deputy Mayor really be the Garbage Dump Killer?

Six of her team were preparing to accompany Amanda to Lower Hutt to find out. A forensics team had been placed on standby alert and half a dozen uniformed men were to surround the address.

"I can't believe it," Janine Harrison declared. "The Deputy Mayor."

Amanda flicked an amused glance at her junior. "You think being a public figure and a murderer are diametrically opposed?"

Predictably, Janine blushed. "I guess history makes nonsense out of that idea. What with Hitler and Stalin, Bokassa, Saddam Hussein . . ."

"John Wayne Gacy had a lot of people fooled with his civic-spirited citizen number," Amanda remarked.

"Why do they do it?"

"God knows . . . Theories are a dime a dozen: contempt for society, hatred of their mothers, attention seeking."

"What do *you* think, Inspector?"

"I think there are only three reasons people kill deliberately — revenge, expedience or pleasure. If it's pleasure, chances are the killer will repeat the experience . . . it's just like any other compulsion."

Janine shuddered. "I hope we get him before he does it again."

"He won't do it again," Amanda said with absolute conviction.

* * * * *

The Wilsons' maid had already let Amanda in
when a hurriedly dressed Harriet Wilson appeared.
She was without makeup and clearly felt at a
disadvantage because of the fact.

"Inspector." She glanced a little wildly past
Amanda to the plainclothes men standing at her
door. "What's happening?"

Amanda took the formal approach, identifying her
colleagues and providing Harriet Wilson with a copy
of the search warrant. "The officers will be as
careful as possible," she assured the flustered
woman. "Now, is Mr. Wilson home?"

Harriet blinked. "No. What's this about?" Her
voice was rising. "I can't have this . . . this invasion.
There's the children to think of."

"Do you have a relative nearby who could take
them for the day? One of my men will drive them
anywhere necessary."

Harriet was staring about her as though she
hadn't heard a word Amanda had said. "I can't
believe this," she declared in an outraged tone. "This
is absolutely scandalous."

Pushing past the hovering maid, Harriet hastened
to the kitchen where several men had spread the
contents of her freezer across the floor and were
loading up bag after bag to be taken to the lab.

"What are you doing?" Harriet was incensed. "I've
only just butchered that!"

A deathly hush fell.

"Please come with me, Harriet," Amanda said in
a conciliatory tone. "We need to talk."

Signaling Janine Harrison, she led Harriet toward

the sitting room, saying, "This is Detective Harrison. She'll come in with us if you don't mind."

Harriet murmured something indistinct. Her hands trembled as she fumbled with the sitting room doors. Before they had closed behind her, she was crying. "I knew this would happen. He hasn't been home for two days, and now ..."

"Harriet, do you have any idea where your husband is?"

She shook her head defeatedly.

"When did you last see him?" Amanda glanced at Janine. The young detective was assiduously taking notes.

"He was here on Friday morning."

"Did he say something about going away?"

Harriet was shaking her head. "Nothing. He just went to work and didn't come home."

"How did you feel about this?"

Harriet looked at Amanda as though she'd taken leave of her senses. "How do you think I feel? He's my husband."

"Harriet, if you were worried about him, why didn't you contact the police?"

"Oh, I'm not worried about *him*," Harriet's voice was shrill. "Mikey's an expert at putting himself first. Anyway —" She rounded suddenly on Amanda. "What's all this about? Has something happened to him?"

"Not that we can report," Amanda said. "But we would like to speak to him. Is there a place he goes for weekends? A friend ..."

Harriet stared at her. There was an odd light in her hazel eyes, the gleam of an idea. "There's the beach house, I suppose."

"You have a beach house?"

"It was Mikey's mother's," Harriet said. "Awfully primitive. I never used it of course, but Mikey goes up there sometimes . . ."

"Where is this, Harriet?"

"Paekakariki. On Ocean View Road."

It was almost too good to be true. "Feel like another drive?" Amanda invited Janine.

Harriet Wilson's idea of primitive was a split-level cedar home with a tennis court and a four-car garage.

Amanda parked the mufti vehicle a few houses down, took the set of keys Harriet offered and told her to wait in the car. Those of the Task Force not engaged in the lengthy business of searching the Wilson's Lower Hutt house were on their way from Wellington Central.

Janine Harrison was clearly champing at the bit. "Let's go," Amanda said.

The house was empty, the air stifling and dust-laden. After methodically scanning each room, they moved to the kitchen. Bracing herself, Amanda opened the fridge. Several cans of Diet Coke occupied the top shelf and decayed lettuce suppurated in the vege bin. There was no freezer.

"Nothing in here," Janine returned from the wash-house. "Except these." She propped a large stack of green plastic trash bags against the kitchen bench.

Through the lace-covered curtains, Amanda

noticed a shell path leading to a large aluminum garden shed at the rear of the property. She stared long and hard and finally realized what was making her skin prickle. Blowflies.

Unlocking the back door, she met Janine's eyes and knew suddenly that her companion would never look so young again.

No amount of professional training and desensitization could prepare you for some sights, Amanda reflected. You could hold your breath, but only for a moment's grace. You could cover your eyes but only when it was too late and your mind was already imprinted with that first hideous impression.

"Oh, God." Janine Harrison was white and shaking.

The inside of the garden shed was an abattoir, its sawdust floor a grisly sea of old congealed blood. The sawdust might have disguised the odor of death once, but not any more. The place smelled foul and metallic. At the far end stood a substantial chest freezer, on which reposed a battered suitcase.

The walls were hung with various hand tools and power saws and in the center of the room was a sawbench oily with absorbed blood.

Sliding her .357 back into its holster, Amanda pulled on latex gloves. "Get back to the car," she told Janine. "And see what the hell is keeping the rest of them. Don't let Harriet come onto the property."

The young woman bolted like a frightened deer

and, steeling herself, Amanda advanced carefully into the carnage. *So this is it,* she thought, *your private slaughterhouse.*

She approached the freezer, and gripping the suitcase on top of it, lifted the lid sufficiently to peer in.

"Hold it right there, Valentine!" a voice exploded behind her. "Arms above your head."

Lowering the lid, Amanda turned to confront Bob Welch. Next to him stood Michael Wilson, his expression feverish with a mixture of fear and excitement. He was holding a gun on a white-faced, handcuffed Janine Harrison.

"Sorry about the welcome," he said with an idiot grin. "We weren't expecting guests."

Impossible, Amanda decided, rapidly assessing her options. Welch had a .38 trained on her and Wilson was shielded by Janine. Even if she could spring a surprise she was uncertain how Janine would respond.

Welch was moving toward her. "You were a fool, coming out here alone," he sneered. "Always the bloody hothead, eh, Valentine."

"Put it down, Bob," Amanda said. "Don't make it any worse for yourself."

Welch laughed nastily. "You're confused about who's in charge. Amazing how a medal and a few headlines can go to someone's head."

"It's not worth it. I know everything, Bob. About both of you. I know about Clarke. I know about the couriers . . ."

"Real smart, aren't you?" Bob placed the barrel of

his gun against her chest and disarmed her, shoving her .357 into his belt.

"The letter was a big mistake, Bob," Amanda said. "We had a suspect but then the letter proved he wasn't our man. Why did you send it? You only succeeded in revealing yourself."

"Shut up, Valentine." He shoved her roughly into the corner of the shed. He grabbed Janine and swung her heavily to the floor, beside Amanda.

"I'll sort these two out," he barked impatiently to Wilson. "Take the money and get out to the car."

Stuffing his gun into his belt, Wilson hoisted the suitcase off the freezer and started toward the door.

"Oh, no you don't!" cried a shrill voice, and Harriet marched into the shed, holding a .22 pistol with both hands. Aiming at her husband's chest she shrieked, "Move and I'll shoot, you bastard."

"Harriet, darling, be sensible." Wilson's voice was a fractured whine.

"You," she shouted at Welch. "Drop that gun and move away from the Inspector or I'll shoot him."

To Amanda's utter astonishment, Welch, his face drawn, did exactly as she said.

"Harriet," Michael was pleading. "There's no need. We're not going to hurt anyone ..."

Harriet laughed, a dry, racking sound. "You hurt *me*! You thought I didn't know. Hah! A wife always knows!"

"It wasn't our idea," Wilson blurted. "It was Chris. He made us do it. We never killed anyone ..."

"That's right, Harriet." Amanda kept her eyes on

Bob Welch. "Chris Clarke killed drug couriers who had itchy feet or big mouths. And he made his mates chop them up and get rid of the pieces. Isn't that right, boys? He wanted to make it look like a serial killer was on the loose."

Sweat was pouring down Wilson's face. "I didn't want to get involved. But we —"

"Shut up!" Welch snapped.

"No, you shut up!" Harriet yelled. "I don't know what else you've been up to." Her eyes flicked around the shed as though seeing it for the first time and her mouth quivered with horror. "You're the one who dragged Mikey into this. You filthy pervert!" She faced Amanda, declaring, "That man seduced my husband! For five whole years!"

Stunned silence fell across the scene. Amanda boggled. Bob Welch was gay? He and Wilson were having an affair? *That* explained why he had disarmed himself — to protect Wilson. Welch's face was ashen. He was staring fixedly at Wilson. Janine looked dumbstruck.

"Mikey tried to stop," Harriet said bitterly. "But that bastard wouldn't leave him alone. He's ruined my life!"

Harriet babbled her story, pouring out what must have been years of resentment. Chris Clarke was the one who told her that the affairs she thought her husband was having with cheap tarts all over town were actually one affair with a *man*. Clarke would leak it to the media if Wilson tried to pull out of their arrangements. He had a big file on Michael Wilson, he boasted. Enough to destroy him. "I told Mikey," Harriet concluded bitterly.

"So your husband killed Chris Clarke?" Amanda asked.

Harriet broke into loud sobs. "It was an accident. He went to get the file off him and to make him see sense. Mikey could have done plenty for Chris Clarke when he became mayor! But he refused."

She glanced down at the gun in her hand and shivered. "I got so angry . . ."

"You were there?" Amanda whispered. Why hadn't she seen it sooner?

Amanda visualized them sitting on the sofa side by side, Harriet and Michael Wilson, confronting Clarke. Clarke dangling Michael Wilson's gay affair under their noses, telling them to shut up or he'd blow the lid on Wilson. Goodbye, Mayoralty. Hello, divorce. She could see Harriet sliding the gun from her handbag, letting him have it while her husband looked on flabbergasted. Michael Wilson would never have killed Clarke. He was making too much money out of him. All he had to do was get rid of the occasional body or two . . . Besides, if the cash-filled suitcase was anything to go by, Wilson and his "buddy" had been planning their own escape.

Harriet, on the other hand, stood to lose everything she held most dear. Respectability, her farcical marriage, the Mayoralty. She had told her husband to ring Bob Welch and tell him he had murdered Clarke, ask for protection.

Harriet suddenly clammed up, her eyes darting to Bob Welch. She was losing it. And Bob Welch was eyeing the guns on the floor.

"It's okay, Harriet," Amanda said, trying to sound soothing.

"No!" Harriet cried. "It's not okay! I was going to be Mayoress. I've even got my civic gown ordered. And now ..." Her voice rose to a high-pitched treble. "It's ruined. All ruined!"

She was pulling the trigger even as Amanda leaped.

A final shot bounced off the aluminum roof as Amanda wrestled the gun from the distraught woman.

Then there was just a soft pattering noise and the sounds from Michael Wilson, crouched over his lover, weeping as the life bled from him.

"I think it's raining," said Janine Harrison.

CHAPTER NINETEEN

Paekakariki Beach is windy and unspoiled. The Tasman Sea pounds restlessly on its golden sands, leaving silky smooth driftwood in great heaps at high tide level. On a hot summer's day, children and dogs frolic around inert adult forms stretched out on enormous beach towels, impervious to the hole in the atmosphere above New Zealand. At lunchtime, men traipse to cars and haul out portable barbecues and white chili-bins, and for a while the beach smells like a sausage pit. By late afternoon, children are crying, dogs are fighting and picnic litter is blowing into the tussock grass.

It wasn't the best time to be on the beach, Amanda conceded, but she strolled anyway. It was still raining lightly, but she had declined Austin Shaw's offer of a coat, or of company.

Are you satisfied? She sent a cosmic message to Chris Clarke. *Was it worth it?*

What had he left behind? Four dead and a wake of misery that seeped as invisibly and destructively as radioactive waste into every life he touched.

Life was cheap to men like Clarke. People were expendable. The Garbage Dump Killer had not been a maniac on a gruesome odyssey of thrill killing. He hadn't been prowling the streets seeking random victims with whom to exercise the power of life or death.

No, Chris Clarke killed for expedience. He killed because people got in his way, and he was able to kill because he had no respect for life. It was a trait shared by every killer — monster or mundane.

Chief Inspector Bailey's office was small and cluttered, its high ceiling freshly painted to cover the smoke stains. The Chief was filling his pipe when Amanda came in.

He lit up and puffed reflectively. "I've read your reports, Valentine. And I've read this." He waved a single typed sheet, lowered his pipe, and stared at her across the sea of paperwork. "There's no shame in asking for some time out, you know. I've had the job go stale on me, too. A good cop recognizes the symptoms and steps out for a spell."

"Sir, it's not that," Amanda said. "I've given it a great deal of thought. It wasn't an easy decision." She ran her fingers into her hair and chewed down on her bottom lip. "I feel like I'm letting you and my men down, sir. But that's not a good enough reason for me to stay."

The Chief nodded, folded his arms and looked beyond Amanda to the view out his narrow windows. It was a blameless summer day, the occasional gull wheeling, fine drifts of cloud pulled like candy floss across the dazzling sky. The Chief pushed her resignation across the desk at her. "I don't want to accept this right now, Valentine. I want you to take some leave, give yourself some time to think it over. You'd be a huge loss to the Force. I'm sure you know that."

"Chief," Amanda said huskily, "when I came out here to New Zealand, you could say I was running away from a lot of things. Time to think it over won't make any difference ... it's already taken me five years to make this decision."

"You're going home, then?"

"Yes, sir."

The Chief clipped the letter to her file. "In that case there's nothing more I can say, except to wish you the very best of luck, Valentine." He got to his feet and extended his hand.

Amanda rose and gripped it firmly. "Sir." She paused on her way out. "Could I ask you one thing? When did you know about Welch?"

The grooves beside his mouth deepened for a

moment and the older man gave her a measuring look. "There's one thing I've learned in many years on the job. The surest way to trap the average criminal is to spot the trap he lays for himself. They all do it, you know." He caught Amanda's dubious expression. "We only had to give them enough room."

"You shifted me out of the picture so Bob Welch could trap himself? Why didn't you tell me?"

"Because I was only guessing."

"You had a hunch?"

The Chief smiled slowly, contemplatively. "Yes. I had a hunch."

A week later, dining with Debby, Amanda consumed her last scallop with a sigh of pleasure. "That really was the best seafood I've ever eaten."

Debby nodded and poured their coffees. "I've got some fantastic news," she said. "I did exactly what you said. I'm forming my own production company and guess who's backing me?"

Amanda felt like her body was turning to ice and any minute it would splinter all over the floor at Debby's feet.

"I don't know," she said hoarsely. "Who?"

"Doug Rollo!" Debby exclaimed. "He was so impressed with my show — the new serious image, that he offered me a PR job. I turned him down of course, but it got me thinking and I faxed a proposal to him."

"Great," Amanda said hollowly.

"Look, I know he's a sleazeball and all that, but

the guy's loaded and underneath it all he's really quite sweet."

"Sweet." Amanda echoed.

"Since I've got to know him better, yes." Debby was starting to sound defensive.

Amanda looked at her sharply. "Are you sleeping with him?"

"Of course not!" Debby looked affronted. "How could you even suggest that!"

Amanda pulled a deep, steadying breath. "I'm sorry. I guess I'm a bit shocked, that's all. It's very sudden."

"So was your decision to go back home," Debby reminded her, and for a moment Amanda glimpsed pain in her eyes. "You never discussed it with me at all. You just decided."

Amanda was silent.

"Can't you just be happy for me," Debby begged. "It's a great opportunity. Doug's got all the top legal talent putting it together, he's giving me total artistic freedom and he's already found me a great apartment in one of his buildings in Auckland." She took Amanda's hand. "Please . . ."

Amanda pressed the slender fingers, lifted them to her mouth to plant a gentle kiss. "It sounds wonderful," she said.

"Of course I want you to come, too," Debby burst out, seemingly flustered. "I mean, now you've given up your job, you're free to do whatever you like, aren't you? You could get a job in Auckland . . ."

"I'm going back home, Debby," Amanda said. "I was kind of hoping you might be interested in a move to New York."

"Oh." Debby studied her nails. "Well, perhaps after I've set up the company and got things going ... maybe then ..."

"It's okay." Amanda slid a hand up to cup Debby's face, tilting it to hers. She kissed her very tenderly. "Let's not make any promises we don't plan to keep. That way we can stay friends."

Debby blinked, returned the kiss and for a long time they simply held each other. Then she pulled back, stared at Amanda and her eyes registered shock, followed quickly by relief. "We're not in love," she finally said. "Or we'd find a way to stay together."

"No," Amanda agreed in a whisper. "We're not in love."

Joe was devouring a fourteen-ounce T-bone. Amanda ordered another Scotch and water. "I've finished in the Mayor's Office," she said.

"Great. So what's the scam?"

"Which one? You know all about Wilson and the marble quarry. Then there's the typist he paid a thousand bucks to, in exchange for her statement that Harvey Perkins molested her. There are all those committee members who pocketed their fees and never questioned what was going on ..."

"And these are the people entrusted to run our city?" Joe sawed into his steak with a resigned groan. "So how can you resign, partner? You just got a commendation. Christ, hang around long enough and you might even get a pay raise."

Amanda grinned. "It's not the job, Joe."

"Personal stuff, huh?" He went red and started shredding his napkin. "You know, Amanda, we've been working together a fair time now ... been through a lot." He cleared his throat. "I want you to know it doesn't make any difference to me if you, er ... Meryl and I, well we're both open-minded people."

Amanda got the general drift. Joe really had been going to that men's group too long.

"I'm gonna miss you, Joe," she said honestly.

Joe pushed his half-eaten meal to one side and groped around in his pockets for a handkerchief.

"Sinus," he explained, as he blew his nose.

Amanda followed suit. "Tears," she said.

CHAPTER TWENTY

Five years. Amanda surveyed the boxes and bags cluttering her sitting room. Five years and not a whole lot to show for it.

Roseanne was in the bedroom stacking the last of the books into a box marked Gay & Lesbian Fair. Amanda stared at her empty house, the piles of boxes, five years of her life wrapped up and ready to be taken back home. Tears welled and as her vision blurred, it was as though Kelly stood before her, large as life, smiling that wonderful smile, her eyes shining with reckless promise, her body warm and waiting.

Amanda blinked, blamed it on the sunlight shafting through her naked windows, the stress of the past month. But Kelly was still there, one hand tantalizingly extended.

In her mind's eye, Amanda took it, allowed herself to be led far away to some grassy place beneath a wide blue sky. Hand-in-hand she walked with Kelly until they came to a small concrete slab. Holding each other, they read the words Amanda had refused to see five years before.

Kelly Delaney O'Conner
1956–1985
beloved daughter of
Ellen and Patrick O'Conner

Amanda felt a searing pain in her chest, the blood rushed in her ears. She wanted to scream at the fates but was voiceless. Tears were coursing down her face and she was shaking all over, crying goodbye to a woman drifting slowly away from her. The woman turned once, waved.

Then Amanda was sobbing in Roseanne's arms, her face buried in Roseanne's shoulder.

"Oh, honey." Roseanne was smoothing her hair, rocking her back and forth. "It's okay to be sad. It's okay to cry." She sank down onto the floor, pulling Amanda with her and cradling her close. "It's really okay." She stroked soothing hands down Amanda's back until the tears finally slowed.

"You'll meet someone else," she said softly. "And

you'll fall in love again ... it's already happened to me six times this year."

Amanda pushed her hair out of her eyes and gave a shaky laugh. "I guess you're right. You never know what's around the corner."

INTRODUCING AMANDA VALENTINE by Rose Beecham.
256 pp. An Amanda Valentine Mystery — 1st in a series.
ISBN 1-56280-021-3 $9.95

UNCERTAIN COMPANIONS by Robbi Sommers. 204 pp.
Steamy, erotic novel.   ISBN 1-56280-17-5   9.95

A TIGER'S HEART by Lauren W. Douglas. 240 pp. Fourth Caitlin
Reece Mystery.   ISBN 1-56280-018-3   9.95

PAPERBACK ROMANCE by Karin Kallmaker. 256 pp. A
delicious romance.   ISBN 1-56280-019-1   9.95

MORTON RIVER VALLEY by Lee Lynch. 304 pp. Lee Lynch at
her best!   ISBN 1-56280-016-7   9.95

LOVE, ZENA BETH by Diane Salvatore. 224 pp. The most talked
about lesbian novel of the nineties!   ISBN 1-56280-015-9   18.95

THE LAVENDER HOUSE MURDER by Nikki Baker. 224 pp. A
Virginia Kelly Mystery. Second in a series.   ISBN 1-56280-012-4   9.95

PASSION BAY by Jennifer Fulton. 224 pp. Passionate romance,
virgin beaches, tropical skies.   ISBN 1-56280-028-0   9.95

STICKS AND STONES by Jackie Calhoun. 208 pp. Contemporary
lesbian lives and loves.   ISBN 1-56280-020-5   9.95

DELIA IRONFOOT by Jeane Harris. 192 pp. Adventure for Delia
and Beth in the Utah mountains.   ISBN 1-56280-014-0   9.95

UNDER THE SOUTHERN CROSS by Claire McNab. 192 pp.
Romantic nights Down Under.   ISBN 1-56280-011-6   9.95

RIVERFINGER WOMEN by Elana Nachman/Dykewomon.
208 pp. Classic Lesbian/feminist novel.   ISBN 1-56280-013-2   8.95

A CERTAIN DISCONTENT by Cleve Boutell. 240 pp. A unique
coterie of women.   ISBN 1-56280-009-4   9.95

GRASSY FLATS by Penny Hayes. 256 pp. Lesbian romance in
the '30s.   ISBN 1-56280-010-8   9.95

A SINGULAR SPY by Amanda K. Williams. 192 pp. 3rd spy novel
featuring Lesbian agent Madison McGuire.   ISBN 1-56280-008-6   8.95

THE END OF APRIL by Penny Sumner. 240 pp. A Victoria Cross
Mystery. First in a series.   ISBN 1-56280-007-8   8.95

A FLIGHT OF ANGELS by Sarah Aldridge. 240 pp. Romance set at
the National Gallery of Art   ISBN 1-56280-001-9   9.95

HOUSTON TOWN by Deborah Powell. 208 pp. A Hollis Carpenter
mystery. Second in a series.   ISBN 1-56280-006-X   8.95

KISS AND TELL by Robbi Sommers. 192 pp. Scorching stories by
the author of *Pleasures*.   ISBN 1-56280-005-1   9.95

STILL WATERS by Pat Welch. 208 pp. Second in the Helen
Black mystery series.   ISBN 0-941483-97-5   8.95

MURDER IS GERMANE by Karen Saum. 224 pp. The 2nd
Brigid Donovan mystery.   ISBN 0-941483-98-3   8.95

TO LOVE AGAIN by Evelyn Kennedy. 208 pp. Wildly
romantic love story.   ISBN 0-941483-85-1   9.95

IN THE GAME by Nikki Baker. 192 pp. A Virginia Kelly
mystery. First in a series.   ISBN 01-56280-004-3   8.95

AVALON by Mary Jane Jones. 256 pp. A Lesbian Arthurian
romance.   ISBN 0-941483-96-7   9.95

STRANDED by Camarin Grae. 320 pp. Entertaining, riveting
adventure.   ISBN 0-941483-99-1   9.95

THE DAUGHTERS OF ARTEMIS by Lauren Wright Douglas.
240 pp. Third Caitlin Reece mystery.   ISBN 0-941483-95-9   8.95

CLEARWATER by Catherine Ennis. 176 pp. Romantic secrets
of a small Louisiana town.   ISBN 0-941483-65-7   8.95

THE HALLELUJAH MURDERS by Dorothy Tell. 176 pp.
Second Poppy Dillworth mystery.   ISBN 0-941483-88-6   8.95

ZETA BASE by Judith Alguire. 208 pp. Lesbian triangle
on a future Earth.   ISBN 0-941483-94-0   9.95

SECOND CHANCE by Jackie Calhoun. 256 pp. Contemporary
Lesbian lives and loves.   ISBN 0-941483-93-2   9.95

MURDER BY TRADITION by Katherine V. Forrest. 288 pp.
A Kate Delafield Mystery. 4th in a series. ISBN 0-941483-89-4   18.95

BENEDICTION by Diane Salvatore. 272 pp. Striking,
contemporary romantic novel.   ISBN 0-941483-90-8   9.95

CALLING RAIN by Karen Marie Christa Minns. 240 pp.
Spellbinding, erotic love story   ISBN 0-941483-87-8   9.95

BLACK IRIS by Jeane Harris. 192 pp. Caroline's hidden past . . .
                                       ISBN 0-941483-68-1   8.95

TOUCHWOOD by Karin Kallmaker. 240 pp. Loving, May/
December romance.   ISBN 0-941483-76-2   8.95

BAYOU CITY SECRETS by Deborah Powell. 224 pp. A Hollis
Carpenter mystery. First in a series. ISBN 0-941483-91-6   8.95

COP OUT by Claire McNab. 208 pp. 4th Det. Insp. Carol Ashton
mystery.   ISBN 0-941483-84-3   9.95

LODESTAR by Phyllis Horn. 224 pp. Romantic, fast-moving
adventure.   ISBN 0-941483-83-5   8.95

THE BEVERLY MALIBU by Katherine V. Forrest. 288 pp. A
Kate Delafield Mystery. 3rd in a series. (HC)   ISBN 0-941483-47-9   16.95
                               Paperback   ISBN 0-941483-48-7   9.95

THAT OLD STUDEBAKER by Lee Lynch. 272 pp. Andy's affair
with Regina and her attachment to her beloved car.
                                             ISBN 0-941483-82-7   9.95

PASSION'S LEGACY by Lori Paige. 224 pp. Sarah is swept into
the arms of Augusta Pym in this delightful historical romance.
                                             ISBN 0-941483-81-9   8.95

THE PROVIDENCE FILE by Amanda Kyle Williams. 256 pp.
Second espionage thriller featuring lesbian agent Madison McGuire
                                             ISBN 0-941483-92-4   8.95

I LEFT MY HEART by Jaye Maiman. 320 pp. A Robin Miller
Mystery. First in a series.   ISBN 0-941483-72-X   9.95

THE PRICE OF SALT by Patricia Highsmith (writing as Claire
Morgan). 288 pp. Classic lesbian novel, first issued in 1952 . . .
acknowledged by its author under her own, very famous, name.
                                             ISBN 1-56280-003-5   8.95

SIDE BY SIDE by Isabel Miller. 256 pp. From beloved author of
Patience and Sarah.   ISBN 0-941483-77-0   8.95

SOUTHBOUND by Sheila Ortiz Taylor. 240 pp. Hilarious sequel
to *Faultline*.   ISBN 0-941483-78-9   8.95

STAYING POWER: LONG TERM LESBIAN COUPLES
by Susan E. Johnson. 352 pp. Joys of coupledom.
                                             ISBN 0-941-483-75-4   12.95

SLICK by Camarin Grae. 304 pp. Exotic, erotic adventure.
                                             ISBN 0-941483-74-6   9.95

NINTH LIFE by Lauren Wright Douglas. 256 pp. A Caitlin
Reece mystery. 2nd in a series.   ISBN 0-941483-50-9   8.95

PLAYERS by Robbi Sommers. 192 pp. Sizzling, erotic novel.
                                             ISBN 0-941483-73-8   8.95

MURDER AT RED ROOK RANCH by Dorothy Tell. 224 pp.
First Poppy Dillworth adventure.   ISBN 0-941483-80-0   8.95

LESBIAN SURVIVAL MANUAL by Rhonda Dicksion.
112 pp. Cartoons!   ISBN 0-941483-71-1   8.95

A ROOM FULL OF WOMEN by Elisabeth Nonas. 256 pp.
Contemporary Lesbian lives.   ISBN 0-941483-69-X   8.95

MURDER IS RELATIVE by Karen Saum. 256 pp. The first
Brigid Donovan mystery.   ISBN 0-941483-70-3   8.95

PRIORITIES by Lynda Lyons 288 pp. Science fiction with
a twist.   ISBN 0-941483-66-5   8.95

THEME FOR DIVERSE INSTRUMENTS by Jane Rule. 208 pp. Powerful romantic lesbian stories. ISBN 0-941483-63-0 8.95

LESBIAN QUERIES by Hertz & Ertman. 112 pp. The questions you were too embarrassed to ask. ISBN 0-941483-67-3 8.95

CLUB 12 by Amanda Kyle Williams. 288 pp. Espionage thriller featuring a lesbian agent! ISBN 0-941483-64-9 8.95

DEATH DOWN UNDER by Claire McNab. 240 pp. 3rd Det. Insp. Carol Ashton mystery. ISBN 0-941483-39-8 9.95

MONTANA FEATHERS by Penny Hayes. 256 pp. Vivian and Elizabeth find love in frontier Montana. ISBN 0-941483-61-4 8.95

CHESAPEAKE PROJECT by Phyllis Horn. 304 pp. Jessie & Meredith in perilous adventure. ISBN 0-941483-58-4 8.95

LIFESTYLES by Jackie Calhoun. 224 pp. Contemporary Lesbian lives and loves. ISBN 0-941483-57-6 8.95

VIRAGO by Karen Marie Christa Minns. 208 pp. Darsen has chosen Ginny. ISBN 0-941483-56-8 8.95

WILDERNESS TREK by Dorothy Tell. 192 pp. Six women on vacation learning "new" skills. ISBN 0-941483-60-6 8.95

MURDER BY THE BOOK by Pat Welch. 256 pp. A Helen Black Mystery. First in a series. ISBN 0-941483-59-2 8.95

BERRIGAN by Vicki P. McConnell. 176 pp. Youthful Lesbian — romantic, idealistic Berrigan. ISBN 0-941483-55-X 8.95

LESBIANS IN GERMANY by Lillian Faderman & B. Eriksson. 128 pp. Fiction, poetry, essays. ISBN 0-941483-62-2 8.95

THERE'S SOMETHING I'VE BEEN MEANING TO TELL YOU Ed. by Loralee MacPike. 288 pp. Gay men and lesbians coming out to their children. ISBN 0-941483-44-4 9.95
 ISBN 0-941483-54-1 16.95

LIFTING BELLY by Gertrude Stein. Ed. by Rebecca Mark. 104 pp. Erotic poetry. ISBN 0-941483-51-7 8.95
 ISBN 0-941483-53-3 14.95

ROSE PENSKI by Roz Perry. 192 pp. Adult lovers in a long-term relationship. ISBN 0-941483-37-1 8.95

AFTER THE FIRE by Jane Rule. 256 pp. Warm, human novel by this incomparable author. ISBN 0-941483-45-2 8.95

SUE SLATE, PRIVATE EYE by Lee Lynch. 176 pp. The gay folk of Peacock Alley are all cats. ISBN 0-941483-52-5 8.95

CHRIS by Randy Salem. 224 pp. Golden oldie. Handsome Chris and her adventures. ISBN 0-941483-42-8 8.95

THREE WOMEN by March Hastings. 232 pp. Golden oldie. A triangle among wealthy sophisticates. ISBN 0-941483-43-6 8.95

RICE AND BEANS by Valeria Taylor. 232 pp. Love and
romance on poverty row.   ISBN 0-941483-41-X   8.95

PLEASURES by Robbi Sommers. 204 pp. Unprecedented
eroticism.   ISBN 0-941483-49-5   8.95

EDGEWISE by Camarin Grae. 372 pp. Spellbinding
adventure.   ISBN 0-941483-19-3   9.95

FATAL REUNION by Claire McNab. 224 pp. 2nd Det. Inspec.
Carol Ashton mystery.   ISBN 0-941483-40-1   8.95

KEEP TO ME STRANGER by Sarah Aldridge. 372 pp. Romance
set in a department store dynasty.   ISBN 0-941483-38-X   9.95

HEARTSCAPE by Sue Gambill. 204 pp. American lesbian in
Portugal.   ISBN 0-941483-33-9   8.95

IN THE BLOOD by Lauren Wright Douglas. 252 pp. Lesbian
science fiction adventure fantasy   ISBN 0-941483-22-3   8.95

THE BEE'S KISS by Shirley Verel. 216 pp. Delicate, delicious
romance.   ISBN 0-941483-36-3   8.95

RAGING MOTHER MOUNTAIN by Pat Emmerson. 264 pp.
Furosa Firechild's adventures in Wonderland.   ISBN 0-941483-35-5   8.95

IN EVERY PORT by Karin Kallmaker. 228 pp. Jessica's sexy,
adventuresome travels.   ISBN 0-941483-37-7   9.95

OF LOVE AND GLORY by Evelyn Kennedy. 192 pp. Exciting
WWII romance.   ISBN 0-941483-32-0   8.95

CLICKING STONES by Nancy Tyler Glenn. 288 pp. Love
transcending time.   ISBN 0-941483-31-2   9.95

SURVIVING SISTERS by Gail Pass. 252 pp. Powerful love
story.   ISBN 0-941483-16-9   8.95

SOUTH OF THE LINE by Catherine Ennis. 216 pp. Civil War
adventure.   ISBN 0-941483-29-0   8.95

WOMAN PLUS WOMAN by Dolores Klaich. 300 pp. Supurb
Lesbian overview.   ISBN 0-941483-28-2   9.95

SLOW DANCING AT MISS POLLY'S by Sheila Ortiz Taylor.
96 pp. Lesbian Poetry   ISBN 0-941483-30-4   7.95

DOUBLE DAUGHTER by Vicki P. McConnell. 216 pp. A Nyla
Wade Mystery, third in the series.   ISBN 0-941483-26-6   8.95

HEAVY GILT by Delores Klaich. 192 pp. Lesbian detective/
disappearing homophobes/upper class gay society.
                                           ISBN 0-941483-25-8   8.95

THE FINER GRAIN by Denise Ohio. 216 pp. Brilliant young
college lesbian novel.   ISBN 0-941483-11-8   8.95

THE AMAZON TRAIL by Lee Lynch. 216 pp. Life, travel & lore
of famous lesbian author.   ISBN 0-941483-27-4   8.95

HIGH CONTRAST by Jessie Lattimore. 264 pp. Women of the
Crystal Palace.   ISBN 0-941483-17-7   8.95

OCTOBER OBSESSION by Meredith More. Josie's rich, secret
Lesbian life.   ISBN 0-941483-18-5   8.95

LESBIAN CROSSROADS by Ruth Baetz. 276 pp. Contemporary
Lesbian lives.   ISBN 0-941483-21-5   9.95

BEFORE STONEWALL: THE MAKING OF A GAY AND
LESBIAN COMMUNITY by Andrea Weiss & Greta Schiller.
96 pp., 25 illus.   ISBN 0-941483-20-7   7.95

WE WALK THE BACK OF THE TIGER by Patricia A. Murphy.
192 pp. Romantic Lesbian novel/beginning women's movement.
                                     ISBN 0-941483-13-4   8.95

SUNDAY'S CHILD by Joyce Bright. 216 pp. Lesbian athletics, at
last the novel about sports.   ISBN 0-941483-12-6   8.95

OSTEN'S BAY by Zenobia N. Vole. 204 pp. Sizzling adventure
romance set on Bonaire.   ISBN 0-941483-15-0   8.95

LESSONS IN MURDER by Claire McNab. 216 pp. 1st Det. Inspec.
Carol Ashton mystery — erotic tension!.   ISBN 0-941483-14-2   8.95

YELLOWTHROAT by Penny Hayes. 240 pp. Margarita, bandit,
kidnaps Julia.   ISBN 0-941483-10-X   8.95

SAPPHISTRY: THE BOOK OF LESBIAN SEXUALITY by
Pat Califia. 3d edition, revised. 208 pp.   ISBN 0-941483-24-X   8.95

CHERISHED LOVE by Evelyn Kennedy. 192 pp. Erotic
Lesbian love story.   ISBN 0-941483-08-8   9.95

LAST SEPTEMBER by Helen R. Hull. 208 pp. Six stories & a
glorious novella.   ISBN 0-941483-09-6   8.95

THE SECRET IN THE BIRD by Camarin Grae. 312 pp. Striking,
psychological suspense novel.   ISBN 0-941483-05-3   8.95

TO THE LIGHTNING by Catherine Ennis. 208 pp. Romantic
Lesbian 'Robinson Crusoe' adventure.   ISBN 0-941483-06-1   8.95

THE OTHER SIDE OF VENUS by Shirley Verel. 224 pp.
Luminous, romantic love story.   ISBN 0-941483-07-X   8.95

DREAMS AND SWORDS by Katherine V. Forrest. 192 pp.
Romantic, erotic, imaginative stories.   ISBN 0-941483-03-7   8.95

MEMORY BOARD by Jane Rule. 336 pp. Memorable novel
about an aging Lesbian couple.   ISBN 0-941483-02-9   9.95

THE ALWAYS ANONYMOUS BEAST by Lauren Wright
Douglas. 224 pp. A Caitlin Reece mystery. First in a series.
                                     ISBN 0-941483-04-5   8.95

SEARCHING FOR SPRING by Patricia A. Murphy. 224 pp.
Novel about the recovery of love.   ISBN 0-941483-00-2   8.95

DUSTY'S QUEEN OF HEARTS DINER by Lee Lynch. 240 pp.
Romantic blue-collar novel.   ISBN 0-941483-01-0   8.95

PARENTS MATTER by Ann Muller. 240 pp. Parents'
relationships with Lesbian daughters and gay sons.
                                           ISBN 0-930044-91-6   9.95

THE PEARLS by Shelley Smith. 176 pp. Passion and fun in
the Caribbean sun.   ISBN 0-930044-93-2   7.95

MAGDALENA by Sarah Aldridge. 352 pp. Epic Lesbian novel
set on three continents.   ISBN 0-930044-99-1   8.95

THE BLACK AND WHITE OF IT by Ann Allen Shockley.
144 pp. Short stories.   ISBN 0-930044-96-7   7.95

SAY JESUS AND COME TO ME by Ann Allen Shockley. 288
pp. Contemporary romance.   ISBN 0-930044-98-3   8.95

LOVING HER by Ann Allen Shockley. 192 pp. Romantic love
story.   ISBN 0-930044-97-5   7.95

MURDER AT THE NIGHTWOOD BAR by Katherine V.
Forrest. 240 pp. A Kate Delafield mystery. Second in a series.
                                           ISBN 0-930044-92-4   9.95

ZOE'S BOOK by Gail Pass. 224 pp. Passionate, obsessive love
story.   ISBN 0-930044-95-9   7.95

WINGED DANCER by Camarin Grae. 228 pp. Erotic Lesbian
adventure story.   ISBN 0-930044-88-6   8.95

PAZ by Camarin Grae. 336 pp. Romantic Lesbian adventurer
with the power to change the world.   ISBN 0-930044-89-4   8.95

SOUL SNATCHER by Camarin Grae. 224 pp. A puzzle, an
adventure, a mystery — Lesbian romance.   ISBN 0-930044-90-8   8.95

THE LOVE OF GOOD WOMEN by Isabel Miller. 224 pp.
Long-awaited new novel by the author of the beloved *Patience
and Sarah.*   ISBN 0-930044-81-9   8.95

THE HOUSE AT PELHAM FALLS by Brenda Weathers. 240
pp. Suspenseful Lesbian ghost story.   ISBN 0-930044-79-7   7.95

HOME IN YOUR HANDS by Lee Lynch. 240 pp. More stories
from the author of *Old Dyke Tales.*   ISBN 0-930044-80-0   7.95

EACH HAND A MAP by Anita Skeen. 112 pp. Real-life poems
that touch us all.   ISBN 0-930044-82-7   6.95

SURPLUS by Sylvia Stevenson. 342 pp. A classic early Lesbian
novel.   ISBN 0-930044-78-9   7.95

PEMBROKE PARK by Michelle Martin. 256 pp. Derring-do
and daring romance in Regency England.   ISBN 0-930044-77-0   7.95

THE LONG TRAIL by Penny Hayes. 248 pp. Vivid adventures
of two women in love in the old west.   ISBN 0-930044-76-2   8.95

HORIZON OF THE HEART by Shelley Smith. 192 pp. Hot
romance in summertime New England.　　ISBN 0-930044-75-4　　7.95

AN EMERGENCE OF GREEN by Katherine V. Forrest. 288
pp. Powerful novel of sexual discovery.　　ISBN 0-930044-69-X　　9.95

THE LESBIAN PERIODICALS INDEX edited by Claire
Potter. 432 pp. Author & subject index.　　ISBN 0-930044-74-6　　29.95

DESERT OF THE HEART by Jane Rule. 224 pp. A classic;
basis for the movie *Desert Hearts*.　　ISBN 0-930044-73-8　　9.95

SPRING FORWARD/FALL BACK by Sheila Ortiz Taylor.
288 pp. Literary novel of timeless love.　　ISBN 0-930044-70-3　　7.95

FOR KEEPS by Elisabeth Nonas. 144 pp. Contemporary novel
about losing and finding love.　　ISBN 0-930044-71-1　　7.95

TORCHLIGHT TO VALHALLA by Gale Wilhelm. 128 pp.
Classic novel by a great Lesbian writer.　　ISBN 0-930044-68-1　　7.95

LESBIAN NUNS: BREAKING SILENCE edited by Rosemary
Curb and Nancy Manahan. 432 pp. Unprecedented autobiographies
of religious life.　　ISBN 0-930044-62-2　　9.95

THE SWASHBUCKLER by Lee Lynch. 288 pp. Colorful novel
set in Greenwich Village in the sixties.　　ISBN 0-930044-66-5　　8.95

MISFORTUNE'S FRIEND by Sarah Aldridge. 320 pp. Historical Lesbian novel set on two continents.　　ISBN 0-930044-67-3　　7.95

A STUDIO OF ONE'S OWN by Ann Stokes. Edited by
Dolores Klaich. 128 pp. Autobiography.　　ISBN 0-930044-64-9　　7.95

SEX VARIANT WOMEN IN LITERATURE by Jeannette
Howard Foster. 448 pp. Literary history.　　ISBN 0-930044-65-7　　8.95

A HOT-EYED MODERATE by Jane Rule. 252 pp. Hard-hitting
essays on gay life; writing; art.　　ISBN 0-930044-57-6　　7.95

INLAND PASSAGE AND OTHER STORIES by Jane Rule.
288 pp. Wide-ranging new collection.　　ISBN 0-930044-56-8　　7.95

WE TOO ARE DRIFTING by Gale Wilhelm. 128 pp. Timeless
Lesbian novel, a masterpiece.　　ISBN 0-930044-61-4　　6.95

AMATEUR CITY by Katherine V. Forrest. 224 pp. A Kate
Delafield mystery. First in a series.　　ISBN 0-930044-55-X　　9.95

THE SOPHIE HOROWITZ STORY by Sarah Schulman. 176
pp. Engaging novel of madcap intrigue.　　ISBN 0-930044-54-1　　7.95

THE YOUNG IN ONE ANOTHER'S ARMS by Jane Rule. 224 pp. Classic
Jane Rule.　　ISBN 0-930044-53-3　　9.95

THE BURNTON WIDOWS by Vickie P. McConnell. 272 pp. A
Nyla Wade mystery, second in the series.　　ISBN 0-930044-52-5　　9.95

OLD DYKE TALES by Lee Lynch. 224 pp. Extraordinary
stories of our diverse Lesbian lives.　　ISBN 0-930044-51-7　　8.95

DAUGHTERS OF A CORAL DAWN by Katherine V. Forrest.
240 pp. Novel set in a Lesbian new world.   ISBN 0-930044-50-9   8.95

AGAINST THE SEASON by Jane Rule. 224 pp. Luminous,
complex novel of interrelationships.   ISBN 0-930044-48-7   8.95

LOVERS IN THE PRESENT AFTERNOON by Kathleen
Fleming. 288 pp. A novel about recovery and growth.
    ISBN 0-930044-46-0   8.95

TOOTHPICK HOUSE by Lee Lynch. 264 pp. Love between
two Lesbians of different classes.   ISBN 0-930044-45-2   7.95

MADAME AURORA by Sarah Aldridge. 256 pp. Historical
novel featuring a charismatic "seer."   ISBN 0-930044-44-4   7.95

CURIOUS WINE by Katherine V. Forrest. 176 pp. Passionate
Lesbian love story, a best-seller.   ISBN 0-930044-43-6   8.95

BLACK LESBIAN IN WHITE AMERICA by Anita Cornwell.
141 pp. Stories, essays, autobiography.   ISBN 0-930044-41-X   7.95

CONTRACT WITH THE WORLD by Jane Rule. 340 pp.
Powerful, panoramic novel of gay life.   ISBN 0-930044-28-2   9.95

MRS. PORTER'S LETTER by Vicki P. McConnell. 224 pp.
The first Nyla Wade mystery.   ISBN 0-930044-29-0   7.95

TO THE CLEVELAND STATION by Carol Anne Douglas.
192 pp. Interracial Lesbian love story.   ISBN 0-930044-27-4   6.95

THE NESTING PLACE by Sarah Aldridge. 224 pp. A
three-woman triangle — love conquers all!   ISBN 0-930044-26-6   7.95

THIS IS NOT FOR YOU by Jane Rule. 284 pp. A letter to a
beloved is also an intricate novel.   ISBN 0-930044-25-8   8.95

FAULTLINE by Sheila Ortiz Taylor. 140 pp. Warm, funny,
literate story of a startling family.   ISBN 0-930044-24-X   6.95

ANNA'S COUNTRY by Elizabeth Lang. 208 pp. A woman
finds her Lesbian identity.   ISBN 0-930044-19-3   8.95

PRISM by Valerie Taylor. 158 pp. A love affair between two
women in their sixties.   ISBN 0-930044-18-5   6.95

THE MARQUISE AND THE NOVICE by Victoria Ramstetter.
108 pp. A Lesbian Gothic novel.   ISBN 0-930044-16-9   6.95

OUTLANDER by Jane Rule. 207 pp. Short stories and essays
by one of our finest writers.   ISBN 0-930044-17-7   8.95

ALL TRUE LOVERS by Sarah Aldridge. 292 pp. Romantic
novel set in the 1930s and 1940s.   ISBN 0-930044-10-X   8.95

A WOMAN APPEARED TO ME by Renee Vivien. 65 pp. A
classic; translated by Jeannette H. Foster.   ISBN 0-930044-06-1   5.00

CYTHEREA'S BREATH by Sarah Aldridge. 240 pp. Romantic
novel about women's entrance into medicine.
    ISBN 0-930044-02-9   6.95

TOTTIE by Sarah Aldridge. 181 pp. Lesbian romance in the
turmoil of the sixties.   ISBN 0-930044-01-0   6.95

THE LATECOMER by Sarah Aldridge. 107 pp. A delicate love
story.   ISBN 0-930044-00-2   6.95

ODD GIRL OUT by Ann Bannon.   ISBN 0-930044-83-5   5.95
I AM A WOMAN 84-3; WOMEN IN THE SHADOWS 85-1;   each
JOURNEY TO A WOMAN 86-X; BEEBO BRINKER 87-8. Golden
oldies about life in Greenwich Village.

JOURNEY TO FULFILLMENT, A WORLD WITHOUT MEN, and   3.95
RETURN TO LESBOS. All by Valerie Taylor   each

These are just a few of the many Naiad Press titles — we are the oldest and
largest lesbian/feminist publishing company in the world. Please request a
complete catalog. We offer personal service; we encourage and welcome direct
mail orders from individuals who have limited access to bookstores carrying
our publications.